# PRAISE FOR *AFTER ZERO*

"A striking, masterfully voiced debut with the haunting force of myth, *After Zero* offers an intimate picture of the healing power of writing and owning one's truth when grief and anxiety isolate us in a world too loud to bear."

—Julie Berry, Printz Honor author of *The Passion of Dolssa*, *All the Truth That's in Me*, and *The Scandalous Sisterhood of Prickwillow Place*

"Collins offers readers a compassionate portrait of selective mutism. Elise is so sensitively drawn; a truly memorable character."

—Sally J. Pla, author of *The Someday Birds* and *Stanley Will Probably Be Fine*

"A powerful and poetic novel about the power of words to shape who we are and who we can be."

—John David Anderson, author of *Posted* and *Ms. Bixby's Last Day*

# ALSO BY CHRISTINA COLLINS

*After Zero*

# THE TOWN WITH
# NO MIRRORS

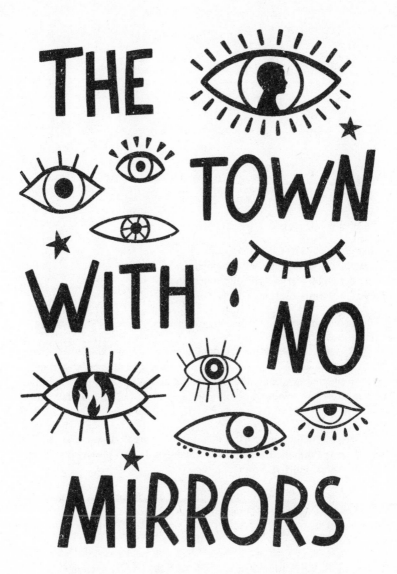

# THE TOWN WITH NO MIRRORS

Christina Collins

sourcebooks
young readers

Copyright © 2023 by Christina Collins
Cover and internal design © 2023 by Sourcebooks
Cover design by Maryn Arreguín/Sourcebooks
Cover illustrations by Tània García

Sourcebooks and the colophon are registered trademarks of Sourcebooks.

Published by Sourcebooks Young Readers, an imprint of Sourcebooks
P.O. Box 4410, Naperville, Illinois 60567–4410
(630) 961-3900
sourcebookskids.com

Cataloging-in-Publication Data is on file with the Library of Congress.

This product conforms to all applicable CPSC and CPSIA standards.

Source of Production: Versa Press, East Peoria, Illinois, USA
Date of Production: November 2022
Run Number: 5027921

Printed and bound in the United States of America.
VP 10 9 8 7 6 5 4 3 2 1

*For Aidan*

# PART I

SU·PER·FI·CIAL

*adjective*

1. of, relating to, or located near a surface

2. external or outward

3. concerned with or comprehending only what is on the surface or obvious

4. shallow; not profound or thorough

# 1

THINK I HAVE A staring problem.

It feels worst here in art class, but also safest. While everyone else's eyes fix on their projects, mine can roam free. Across from me, Malorie Windleson picks her nose while she draws; it looks pointier than ever today, and a new red spot gleams on its tip. Next to her, Ricky Sanchez grins at whatever he's drawing, revealing the gap between his front teeth; has it widened since yesterday? Beyond him, Hal Gotwell yawns, and the cinnamon-colored specks on his cheeks stretch and shift; I swear they've multiplied since math class this morning.

My eyes move on, scanning my other classmates: mainly bent heads, but at some angles I can see faces. That's what fascinates me most—faces.

I wonder if mine looks like any of theirs.

"Okay, stop what you're doing."

I jerk my gaze to the front of the room. Did I give myself

away somehow? Did I stare too long? I should have known. Mr. Huttle suspects me—senses my Superficial thoughts...

"Time for partner critiques," he announces.

He's looking at the clock, not at me. My muscles loosen a little. False alarm.

Still, I need to be more careful.

"You all know the drill," he says. "Turn to the person next to you."

I look first to my right, where Olive is turning to Jill. That shouldn't surprise me. She's been choosing Jill over me for a while now. It's probably for the best; Olive's drawing a unicorn again. She has unicorn fever. But to each their own, because this week we can draw any subject we want, as long as it incorporates shading. Well, any subject but one, of course.

"Looks like you're stuck with me," says a voice on my left.

I turn toward Noah Spinsky. I guess I don't mind getting him as a partner. Everyone else gives only nice feedback so that they'll get the same in return, but I can trust Noah to be honest.

"An apple?" He raises an eyebrow. "Wow. Exciting subject matter."

Sometimes too honest.

"You're one to talk." I point at his drawing. "Another sunset? How imaginative."

"It's a sun*rise*, thank you very much."

"Right." I grin. "My bad."

The truth is it's fine by me if he thinks I only draw boring, ordinary things. It's safer if people think that—they won't suspect me.

"Anyway." Noah sighs. "Your apple still looks better than anything I could draw. You could draw a dot and still be the best artist in the class."

"I'm not the best." My cheeks burn. Are they reddening like Alice Flynn's do when Mr. Huttle calls on her? No—*Bad Thought*.

"Then why did Mr. Huttle call you that last week? I heard him telling Principal Gladder."

"You did?"

"Don't let it get to your head." Noah leans back in his chair. "Now, should we talk about yours first or mine?"

"Yours," I say, wanting to get the attention off me.

"Yeah, let's save the best for last."

"That's not what I—"

"Break it to me gently." He turns his drawing toward me. "How bad is it?"

I study the drawing: a basic sunrise, with hills, a little house, a semicircle on the horizon, and lines for sunrays. I try not to cringe at the M-shaped birds in the sky. "It's good—I like that you included birds," I say, because I always start with a compliment.

"But?"

"But maybe they could be more...lifelike."

He slouches a little. "Okay. What else?"

"Well..." I search for something to praise; I don't want to make him slouch even more. But I find myself at a loss. "It's really nice overall," I say. "If you wanted, you could add some shadow and dark tones to the hills. Give them more dimension..."

I can't help noticing he's staring at me now while I talk. Which is normal, I know—to look at someone when they're speaking. It's one of the few times staring is appropriate. But his Pop Eyes are fixed somewhere near my nose, threatening to pop right out of their sockets. That's what I call them in my head—Pop Eyes—because they seem almost too big for his eyelids. Now especially.

"More dimension and, um..." I stammer, losing my train of thought. I try to focus on Noah's sunrise. The hills, the M-shaped birds... But I still feel him staring at me. I can dish it out, but apparently I can't take it. What does he see that's so eye-popping?

"Uh, Zailey?" He shifts in his seat. "Are you okay?"

My stomach flips. "Yeah, why?"

"There's something on your..." He clears his throat. "You're kind of bleeding."

"Bleeding?" As my mouth moves, something tickles my top lip. My fingers fly up—and then come away dark red. Oh.

We've always been told that the only time it's okay to talk about someone's appearance is if there's a medical reason. And in that case, you can always find a non-Superficial way to phrase it. I guess that was Noah's way.

"I'll get tissues." Noah leaps up and grabs the Kleenex box on Mr. Huttle's desk.

"Everything okay over there?" Mr. Huttle frowns as Noah hurries back to me.

"Just a nosebleed," I mutter, pulling a bunch of tissues out of the box. I hold them under my nose and pinch my nostrils with my other hand. Noah isn't the only one staring at me now; the whole class is. My cheeks go hot again. The nosebleed is nothing, but the staring—that's what makes me squirm. I need to get away from it.

"You'd better go to the nurse's office, Zailey," Mr. Huttle says, granting my wish. "Can someone walk her there?"

Noah starts to answer, but I push back my chair. "I'm fine. Really. I can go on my own." My pinched nose muffles my voice. Someone snickers—Jill?—but I don't look.

"Are you sure?" Mr. Huttle asks.

I nod and hurry out the door before he can question me further. I exhale in the empty hall.

The nurse's office is all the way on the other side of the school, so I stop in the closest bathroom first. I turn on the sink, and the water comes spurting out, cold. I rinse the blood off my fingers and cup some water in my hands. It looks whitish today, almost like milk—I guess they've been pumping it extra cloudy. I splash it on my nose and grab a wad of paper towels to stuff up my nostrils as I walk to the nurse's office.

There are two ways to get there: I can either walk through the halls all the way to the other side of the school or cut through the courtyard. The first would mean I don't have to leave the air-conditioning, but the second would save me a few minutes—and a walk past Principal Gladder's office. Not that I'm scared of her or anything. *Scared* is a drastic word. But why wouldn't I take a shortcut if I have that option?

I head out the door to the courtyard. I'm already sweating by the time I pass the picnic benches. Voices rumble nearby. Is one of the younger grades having class outside? It seems too hot for that. It's always too hot for that. Even the breeze I feel now makes little difference. But that's the Southwest for you, as Grandma sometimes says. Not that I have any point of comparison. I round the corner where the school's brick wall leads to another section of the courtyard—and freeze. A group stands at the far end: a semicircle of backs facing me. Hair spills down some of the backs. I gasp a little. Outsiders.

Principal Gladder's assistant, Ms. Mohill, is standing in front of them, talking and gesturing with her hands, but I'm too far away to hear what she's saying. I should go before she looks my way... But now she's turning to point at THE FOUNDING STORY OF GLADDER HILL, engraved in the plaque on the wall behind her, so I let myself stare a little longer. I squint. Two of the outsiders are tall—adults—and the rest are shorter. The short ones must be kids, though from here it's hard to be sure. There are at least ten of them.

My stomach dances at the thought: ten new faces. I haven't seen a new one since Joy Torrez's baby brother was born six months ago. And before that, not since a tour group came last summer—parents-to-be who wanted to join our waiting list and raise their kids here. I didn't have a good view of that group either, though I could see the protruding bellies. I see none now.

As the breeze picks up, a girl at the back of the group sneezes. A piece of paper slips from her hand. She turns to snatch it, but the wind beats her to it, whipping it away from her.

Toward me.

The girl starts to chase it. I scuttle backward until I'm around the corner and out of sight. Holding my breath, I watch the cement in front of me. I should go back inside. I should mind my own business...

The piece of paper prances into view. It seems rude to just watch it instead of helping.

Plus, it might blow out of reach if I'm not quick, and then I'll have lost my chance to be more than a spectator.

I step forward and snatch it up.

**Life in Gladder Hill**, the leaflet says at the top. There's more text in smaller print, but the girl reaches me before I have time to read it.

"Oh—thanks for catching that," she pants. I take her in: round cheeks, thick eyelashes, a long nose with a brown dot on one side. There's a strange blue tint to her eyelids, and her lips are pinker and shinier than I knew lips could be. Things hang from her ears: glinting ornaments with little beads, peeking through hair that hangs around her face in a brown mass, so unlike the buzz cuts we all have here.

"No problem," I mumble, handing her the leaflet. She smiles, and her top teeth surprise me; a shiny threadlike piece runs across them, linking little squares on each tooth. I know I'm staring, but I can't help it. It's not every day I get to see a new face. I want to memorize this one—lock it inside my head to go over later. It's completely different from the hundred other faces in Gladder Hill, and yet there's a bit of Emily Brentworth around the eyes, and a touch of Ms. Koy in the nose...

"I'm Beryl," she says.

"I'm Zailey." I remember I'm holding a bloody paper towel and hide it in my fist behind my back, hoping my nose has stopped bleeding. "Are you on a tour?"

She nods. "Well, a field trip. Do you live here?"

"Yeah."

Her eyes widen—green eyes. "Wow, that must be weird."

I frown. "Not really." I glance down at her shirt. It's tight. I didn't even know they made shirts that fit like that. Orange words sweep across the front: *Barkbee Middle School Girls' Soccer.*

"You're from Barkbee?" I blurt. All I know about Barkbee is that it's the closest town to us, where most of our supplies come from. That's all adults have told us about it—aside from the fact that most people are unhappy there, just like everywhere else outside Gladder Hill's gates. I want to ask Beryl a million more questions. How many people are there in Barkbee? How many faces? Are they all different like they are here? But those are Bad Thoughts, so I keep them to myself.

"Yep," Beryl says. "Our social studies teacher's been dying to take us here. She's even making us miss a pep rally—those are always super fun. But she kept saying this trip's more important and we'll find it inspiring and stuff."

"Oh. So what do you think?"

Beryl looks around the courtyard and past my shoulder, as if hoping there's more to see. She shrugs. "It's cute."

*Cute?* That must be Barkbee lingo. Before I can ask, she adds, "But not what I expected. I thought you guys would be like the Amish or something." She grins, wider than before, revealing those shiny linked squares on her teeth again. A little dent appears in one of her cheeks. I've noticed how that happens to a few other people when they smile—Maggie Kirkman, Ricky Sanchez, Gemma Greco. I don't think it happens to me—not from what my fingers can tell anyway.

"The Amish?" I frown.

"Can I get a pic with you? Oh, and my mom wanted me to get one with Felicity Gladder. Is she around?"

"Principal Gladder?" Kids never call her by her first name.

"Yeah." Beryl reaches into her pocket and then pauses. "Oh, wait." She puffs out her cheeks. "They wouldn't let us bring our phones. I don't know how you stand all the rules. I mean, they wouldn't even let me wear *sunglasses*."

I hesitate. I've never had so many questions spinning through my head. Why would she lug a phone around with her? And now I want to ask what sunglasses are, but I assume from the name that they're made of glass—one of our banned materials. Something we shouldn't be talking about. Doesn't she know she shouldn't be talking about it?

"But my teacher says it's all for a good cause." Beryl studies me for a few seconds, and I fidget. Then she leans toward me, lowering her voice. "Is it true no one here knows what they look like?"

My pulse quickens. "You shouldn't talk about that," I whisper.

"But it doesn't seem fair." Beryl shakes her head. "I mean, don't you have the right to know—"

"Excuse me." Ms. Mohill appears behind Beryl, making

us both jump. Today she's wearing one of those T-shirts with our motto in big green letters: *Everyone's gladder in Gladder Hill.* "Young lady, I said not to leave the group. And Zailey, you should be in class."

"Sorry, I was just heading to the nurse," I stammer. "I got a nosebleed."

Ms. Mohill's eyes narrow and dart over me, maybe looking for proof, for blood, but she doesn't let on if she sees any. Is she going to tell Principal Gladder on me? "Well, you can go through the other door," she says, pointing at a door to my right, in the opposite direction of the tour group. The long way to the nurse.

I nod and exchange a glance with Beryl. She mouths *bye* before I turn and hurry toward the door. As I open it, I dare one last glance over my shoulder. But Beryl has already disappeared around the corner with Ms. Mohill. She's gone, her face too—though in my mind it remains: a memento, a keepsake, stored now with the other faces of Gladder Hill. Other faces are all I have to go on when it comes to certain questions in my head. Other faces can tell me what might be possible for my own.

And now here's a new possibility.

# 2

DON'T TELL ANYONE ABOUT the tour. I say nothing to the nurse, who lets me stay in her office till the next bell, even though my nose stopped bleeding. I say nothing to the janitor, who greets me on the long way back through the halls. And when I get to Mr. Wallus's classroom, I say nothing to any of my classmates, even though I'm dying to tell someone about the tour—about Beryl and our conversation.

The trouble is there's no one I can trust to tell. I glance over at Olive, who's chatting away to Jill. I used to think I could tell Olive everything, but that was when we were best friends. And the last time I confided in her, it didn't go well. I still remember her reaction when I asked her if she ever studied her shadow, like I'd done sometimes. Her eyes got all wide, rivaling Noah's Pop Eyes, and she backed away from me like I was some wild animal who might bite her and infect her with my Bad Thoughts. She threatened to tell Principal Gladder what I said, and though she never did, I've been careful since then about everything I say and who I say it to. Sometimes I wonder if *that's* what did it—if that's what made her like me less and Jill more. Probably anyone would react that way to what I said. Everyone else in Gladder Hill is normal, doesn't have Superficial thoughts, and doesn't want to know anyone with Superficial thoughts. So, if I'd like to have friends, clearly I need to keep those thoughts to myself.

"How'd it go with the nurse?" Noah asks, taking the desk next to me.

He's the only person who's bothered to ask so far. It occurs to me he might be the closest thing I have to a friend at the moment, though we've never hung out outside of school, and he already has friends—he's always skateboarding around town with Tony Franco and Jen Rosenthal. He's just being polite, but I guess I'll take what I can get.

"The bleeding stopped before I got there," I tell him. "Anticlimactic, right?"

"Well, in other news, you made my drawing more interesting."

"What do you mean?" I wonder if he took my advice about the birds.

He pulls his drawing out of a folder. "Turns out the house on the hill is a crime scene."

He waits as I study the drawing. I spot a splotch of red on the little house—a drop of blood. I raise my eyebrows and look back at Noah. We burst into laughter. Olive pauses her chat with Jill and glances over at us. Part of me hopes she's jealous.

Mr. Wallus strolls in now and starts class, jumping into a lecture on metaphors and similes and literary devices. I notice he has something stuck in his teeth: spinach, maybe? Obviously no one will point this out to him. He'll go around all day like that.

In spite of myself, I slide my tongue across my own teeth, feeling for any food stuck there.

I start to take notes, but like always, the notes turn into doodles: clouds and mountain peaks and more apples. For better or for worse, this classroom is not staring-friendly; Mr. Wallus has set up the desks in straight rows, not angled like they are in the art room, so my view is mostly the backs of heads. Something catches my eye on the floor. I glance down to where the overhead light casts a shadow. A strange, boxy shape.

*Is it true no one here knows what they look like?*

I try to focus on the lecture, but my mind wanders back to the tour, back to Beryl, back to her question. I tilt my head, and the shape on the floor moves. I know the shadow must be mine because it imitates my motions, as reflections are rumored to do. It answers some questions, like how long my neck is: not long at all. Or what shape my head is: more squarish than round. But other questions it can't answer.

I look down toward my lap and pretend to lick my lips. My tongue flashes into view; I can just see its pink edge. Next, I pretend to itch the bottom of my nose, and as I do, I push it upward for a moment, glimpsing its blurred tip. That's where it ends. That's where I reach the Uncrossable Boundary. My eyes can't access the rest, and that's the way it is. There are parts of me I'll never fully know.

And I don't care about not knowing, I remind myself. Gladder Hill kids don't care. We've been taught from the beginning: Any concern for the human surface, even your own, is wrong. Right up there with stealing, cheating, lying, and all that sort of stuff. Us kids are all in the same boat. Mick Scalini doesn't know his teeth are yellow, just like Jen Rosenthal doesn't know she has that brown mark above her left eyebrow, just like Noah doesn't know he has Pop Eyes. Just like I don't know if my face has any of those distinctions or different ones entirely. And I don't care about not knowing.

Mr. Wallus says something about a quiz tomorrow—something I should be writing down. I look at my notebook and almost gasp. At some point I must have stopped doodling stars and mountains and apples, because there are other things there now.

Two eyes. A nose. The start of a mouth.

I clamp my hand over them, my heart hammering. I look up just as Noah's head turns away at the desk next to me. Did he see what I drew?

I watch him out of the corner of my eye and try not to panic. He seems to be taking notes as if nothing happened.

Still, I don't move my hand for a long time, even as the sweat from my palm seeps onto the paper. Hopefully it will smudge the ink. Why did I have to use a pen today and not a pencil?

Eventually I close my notebook over my hand and then slip my hand out. Noah doesn't seem to react.

Maybe my secret is still safe.

I waste no time after the last bell, hurrying to my locker and then toward the front doors.

"Oh, Zailey?"

My body stiffens. I look up to find Principal Gladder coming out of the copy room. "Can I see you in my office for a minute?"

A feeling of doom crashes over me. Could Noah have tattled already?

"Sure," I squeak, because it's not like I can say no to the principal. That alone would confirm my guilt.

I follow Principal Gladder around the corner, past Ms. Mohill's office, and into her own office, all too aware of the eyes, the nose, and the start of a mouth hiding in the bag on my shoulder. I try to remember the last time someone got in trouble for Superficiality. It used to happen now and then when we were younger, and the punishment was usually the same as for any misbehavior: you'd get put in the corner or sent to the principal's office, depending on how badly you crossed the line. There was only one serious time I can remember, when Jesse Lowell did something Superficial enough that Principal Gladder pulled him out of classes for a week and made him take more of those interiority lessons we'd already had in kindergarten and first grade. He'd asked Ms. Mohill why she had two chins.

But that was the third grade, and I can't remember a time since then when someone my age has gotten in trouble for that sort of thing. Kind of like the way kids eventually stop crying and whining all the time; they reach a point where they understand it's inappropriate behavior.

So, if I were to get in trouble now, when I'm supposed

to know better—us seventh graders are the oldest kids in Gladder Hill, after all—it would be beyond embarrassing. Who knows what my punishment would even be?

"How are your classes going?" Principal Gladder asks, sitting down at her desk and gesturing for me to take the chair opposite her. Small talk before the big question. She might as well mention the weather. Why can't she cut to the point and save me the suspense?

"Good," I say, trying to make eye contact but failing. Some people worship Principal Gladder, especially the adults— especially Grandma. She's their hero. I'm not saying I don't like her...but she sort of intimidates me. I glance around her office. I've only been in here a few times, for student conferences, and the last time was a year ago, but I can tell she's rearranged a few things. Her American Humanitarian Award plaque used to hang on the wall facing her; now it's behind her desk, where visitors like me can see it better. Her poster with our motto—"Everyone's gladder in Gladder Hill"—still hangs on that wall, but it's higher now, above a poster of the Nourish & Flourish food pyramid that's also in the nurse's office and the lunchroom. A new cactus plant grows in a pot next to her desk, and the books and folders on her shelves sit neatly and evenly organized. Much like the parts of her face.

*Bad Thought. Bad Thought.*

I shouldn't be thinking Superficial things in front of her, of all people. Maybe she can detect them—who knows? I wouldn't be surprised if she has a sixth sense. But it's hard to not observe her or anyone's face when I'm, well, face-to-face with it. Hers is—how do I put this?—boring to look at. It's hard to pinpoint why. Some faces are all angles, almost pointy, like Grandma's. Others are round, with hardly any angles at all, like Mr. Wallus's. Principal Gladder's is somewhere in the middle of that spectrum, and its whole surface is plain—not a speck, not a spot, not a dot, not a mark.

I wonder if she knows any of this. She must know, from before. She didn't grow up in Gladder Hill, after all.

"Sounds like art is still your best subject," she says.

Oh no. I brace myself. Here it comes.

"Mr. Huttle says you're one of his top students."

I stare at her. I guess Noah was telling the truth about that, but I don't know if it's something to be proud of. Sure, I've always liked art more than other subjects, but the class itself is a joke—one scant hour per week with Mr. Huttle, who seems more interested in the other classes he teaches, like science and gym.

But I don't say anything in case this is a trap.

"And you're enjoying your three extracurriculars this year..." She glances down at a sheet of paper in front of her. "String orchestra, Ultimate Frisbee, and Rubik's Cube club?"

That's it? She's changing the subject?

I nod.

"And how's your grandma? Doing well, I hope?"

"Yeah, she's good."

"Glad to hear it." She clears her throat and shuffles some papers around on her desk. "Ms. Mohill said you met one of the tourists today. Did she have anything interesting to say?" Her voice is casual—maybe too casual.

"No," I lie.

"What did you two talk about?"

"Not much. I just picked up the paper she dropped, and she said thanks."

Principal Gladder nods, though I don't know if she believes me. She's hard to read. That's another thing I've noticed about faces: sometimes they give you cues, clues about what's being said—a lack of eye contact, a twitching mouth, a crease between the eyes... But other times, like now with Principal Gladder, faces keep themselves still, straight, neutral, offering no help whatsoever. Those faces frustrate me.

"It's just, we need to be careful talking to people who

live outside of Gladder Hill." She folds her hands on her desk. "They might say things or give you ideas that could undo all the good work we've been doing here with you kids."

I nod, both relieved and confused by the direction of the conversation. "I promise I won't talk to anyone next time."

"Oh, I doubt there'll be a next time."

I sink in my seat a little. No more tours? They're the only way I can see new faces. But I can't tell her that. Not that it matters, if she already suspects my Superficiality. I hold my breath and wait for her to move on to the real reason I'm here: a student has reported me—has seen me drawing human features, the one subject that's forbidden from art in school, in all of Gladder Hill...

"Well, thanks for stopping in." She glances at the clock on the wall. "Tell your grandma I say hi, okay?"

I blink. "Okay."

"You can close the door on your way out."

I pick up my schoolbag and leave the office. Well, that went better than expected.

As I close the door behind me, I glimpse Principal Gladder one last time, opening her day planner, tapping her pen against the desk. And I can't help wondering, as I sometimes do, about Principal Gladder's past.

Adults never tell us kids much, so the most we know is that she used to be famous in the outside world, before she founded Gladder Hill. Famous and rich—I guess that helped her create this place. A *philanthropist*, Grandma called her once. Or was it *anthropologist*? I always get the two confused.

# 3

TWENTY-EIGHT MINUTES. THAT'S HOW long it takes to cross from one end of Gladder Hill to the other by foot. By bike it's more like fifteen, but I don't have a bike—maybe for my thirteenth birthday—and either way, sweat usually soaks me in seconds. I'm already soaked, thanks to the visit with Principal Gladder, so stepping outside adds a whole other layer.

I head down Main Street and wave to Mr. Mackafee as he sweeps outside the general store. I pet Tutu, the calico cat that always lounges outside the dentist's office, even though she belongs to the chiropractor. I've drawn Tutu a few times because I love all her colors and any excuse to use my colored pencils—and because drawing animals is allowed.

Next, I head past the police and fire station, which is quiet as usual. Officer Jenkins is probably dozing off inside; he never has much to do.

A golf cart hums past me—a four-seater with Mr.

Aberdeen at the wheel, driving the Romero sisters, probably to the town hall to play bingo with the other old people. I wave at them before turning off Main Street and heading down Mojave Lane. I glance at the Edelmeyer family's house, with all the toys scattered out front and their cart parked in the drive. And then Mr. Grinwold's bungalow, with all the pinwheels lining the walkway, twirling in the breeze. Mr. Grinwold is out front planting some new flowers, so we exchange hellos. He spends most afternoons gardening or decorating his front yard, and I don't blame him. It's easy to get bored in Gladder Hill if you don't have a hobby.

And yet no one seems to leave.

As I head up the hill, I can only think of a few instances when an adult—always an adult—had to leave for a few days. A funeral...a wedding... Most adults don't consider events like that worth leaving for though; a card or a gift or a preapproved phone call will do. It's too risky—the things you could be exposed to, the way they could undo the progress you've made in Gladder Hill. That's what Grandma says anyway. I have no idea what it's like out there—aside from what I can see from the viewpoint.

I crest the hill now. I always stop here after school. It's my favorite place in Gladder Hill. It's a bit out of the way, but it's worth it. No one else is ever here, so I can look out at the world without anyone bothering me. Of course it's the same view every time—sagebrush and trees and mountains stretching to the south, and fields and roads and a winding strip of river reaching toward the north, leading to places I can't go till I'm eighteen. Only five and a half more years.

Only a lifetime.

I sigh and head down the other side of the hill, then onto Suncup Drive until I reach my house. I know Grandma is home, because towels are hanging out to dry.

I swipe my key card, and the air-conditioning envelops me as I walk through the door—one of the best feelings. "Hey, kiddo," Grandma says. She looks up from the kitchen table, where she's doing a word search puzzle.

"How was work?" I slip my backpack off.

"Slow day at the pharmacy, but I'm not complaining." Grandma smiles. "How was school?"

"Fine." I shrug, deciding it's best not to mention the tour or my visit to Principal Gladder's office. I grab a banana from the fruit basket and sit next to her.

"This is a hard one." She circles a word in her puzzle. "Only found two so far."

I glance over at the page. "I see another one."

"Don't tell me." She sucks in her breath, her eyes searching the grid of letters.

I bite into my banana and wait for her to find the word: CURIOUS. She circles other words as she leans forward, squinting at the page.

"Why are you squinting?" I ask.

She chuckles. "Just getting old, I guess."

"Why don't you wear contact lenses?"

"You know I hate putting things in my eyes."

"What about laser eye surgery?"

"And have a machine slice my eyeballs?" She shudders. "No, thanks."

I'll admit that doesn't appeal to me either. But everyone with vision problems in Gladder Hill either wears contacts or gets laser eye surgery at our vision center, so I never wondered what would happen if you couldn't do either. I think of being unable to see. Unable to draw. My skin prickles. "There's really no other option?" I ask.

"Not here," Grandma says, studying her puzzle.

I raise an eyebrow.

"Doesn't matter though, kiddo." Grandma clicks her pen shut and then open. "I'm still better off than anyone outside Gladder Hill. We all are."

*Outside Gladder Hill.*

The phrase sends tingles through my body. Because what Grandma doesn't know is that I have a memory—or at least a vision—of a place I've never seen in Gladder Hill. Every now and then, when I glance at the kitchen or bathroom floor, it floats into my mind: octagonal floor tiles. White ones outlined with orange, and inside each, orange and yellow petals and black flourishes. I don't know where the tiles are, or if they even exist in a real place, but I know they aren't here in Gladder Hill.

I haven't worked up the courage to ask Grandma about them yet.

"Don't worry, my eyesight's fine," she's saying. I must seem concerned, because she smiles and leans toward me. "Besides, I could live without my sight. It's you I couldn't live without." She boops my nose, her face close to mine. Her eyes close to mine. I glimpse something in them, another face, teeny-tiny, one in each pupil, barely there. Barely detectable.

Grandma leans back in her seat again, taking the face with her. I clear my throat and look away. Moments like these happen now and then, but I never mention the teeny face. She might stop coming close like that, and I might never get a better look.

Does she see a face too, when she looks into my eyes?

With her bad eyesight, maybe not.

She squints down at her puzzle now and taps her pen against her chin. "Ah-ha." She grins and circles another word—still not CURIOUS.

I finish my banana and retreat to my room. There's plenty of homework to do—an essay for English, a lab report, math problems... But when I open my English notebook, eyes stare back at me.

Right where I left them.

The eyes, the nose, the start of a mouth. The reason I was hurrying home in the first place.

I should destroy them, shred them, at least blot them out.

I glance back at my door, making sure it's closed. I reach for a pencil.

I bring the pencil tip to the paper and finish the mouth, curving the lips up at one side.

The next thing I know, I'm adjusting the nose, and adding a dot on the side, and drawing a dent near the mouth, and then lines for cheekbones, jaws, a chin. Strokes for eyebrows. As I move the pencil, the outline takes shape—gains details here and there. It's not till I'm finished that I realize who it is.

The tour girl, Beryl, smiles back at me, linked squares on her teeth and all.

Heart pounding, I check my door again and rip the page out. It looks a lot like her, in my opinion—not an exact likeness, but close. I grin in spite of myself, feeling like a magician. Like I conjured Beryl out of nowhere with my pencil—my magic wand.

I've noticed I can store things in my mind—visual things, in detail—for a short while after looking at something even once. It's how I drew that apple in art class without a live model, and how I sketch birds that fly away before I've had a chance to pull out my sketchbook.

And how I've done all the drawings in my collection.

Mr. Huttle once suggested I have an eidetic memory. I don't know if that's true, but I do know that Beryl's face was so vivid in my mind that I had to get her down on paper before she grew fuzzy. It's not like I'll be seeing her again tomorrow to refresh my memory. Her face was time sensitive.

I get on my knees and lift the side of my comforter and then my mattress, feeling around until I find it—there. I pull out the pocket-size sketchbook and bring it to my desk. I flip to a blank page and use a glue stick to paste Beryl's face onto it.

I number the sketch and sit back. Fifty-one. That's how many faces I've got now. I realize with a little gasp that I'm halfway through. Another fifty-one to go before I've drawn every face in Gladder Hill. Except my own, of course. My stomach dances. I wonder how long it will take me.

I skim back through the other pages now. Mr. Wallus, with his big ears and spinach teeth... Olive, with her long forehead and heart-shaped face... Principal Gladder, Malorie Windleson, Ricky Sanchez...all the way to the first one I drew a couple of months ago: the creases and lines, the curved nose, the pointed chin—Grandma.

"Kiddo?"

I jump.

"Can you come help with dinner?" Grandma calls from the other side of my door.

"One sec," I call back.

I shut the sketchbook and slip it back under the mattress, pushing it as far toward the center as I can reach. Then I drop the mattress and smooth the comforter over the side, pulling it extra far down. Because one thing's for sure: No one can know about my face collection. Not even Grandma.

Especially not Grandma.

# 4

I GO BY TWO NAMES, and two names only: Zailey or (if I'm in trouble) Azalea. So I don't know who Grandma's talking to when she says, "Sierra, come taste this."

But I'm the only other person in the house.

"Huh?" I stare at Grandma's back from the kitchen table, where I'm doing homework.

She stands by the stove, stirring a bowl of homemade salsa with a wooden spoon while two omelets sizzle on skillets. "Taste the salsa for me. Not sure if I put enough cilantro and garlic in."

"You called me Sierra," I say.

The spoon freezes in her hand. I wish I could see her face from here. "I did?" She laughs, a little too loudly. "Oops, silly me."

Curiosity bubbles up in me. I remember how she called me Sierra once before, a couple of years ago. How she averted her eyes, mumbled, "Zailey, I mean," and pretended it never happened. How I pretended too.

But this time I'm older—and feeling bolder.

I get up and take the spoon from Grandma, tasting the salsa. "Mm. Perfect."

"Phew."

I lean on the counter. "So who's Sierra?"

Grandma picks up a plate without looking at me and flops an omelet onto it. "Oh. That was the name of a dog I had. Before Gladder Hill."

"You confused me with a dog?"

"I had her a long time." She sprinkles veggies on the omelet that's still cooking. "Don't worry, you smell much nicer than a dog. Could you set the table, please? Dinner's almost ready."

I clear away my homework and set out the place mats, utensils, plates, and cups, all while trying not to lose the nerve to ask more questions. As we sit down to our breakfast for dinner—upside-down day, Grandma calls it—I keep thinking of those words she said. *Before Gladder Hill.* And my vision—my memory?—of octagonal floor tiles.

"Why aren't you eating?" Grandma's voice breaks my thoughts apart, and I realize I'm picking at my omelet. Grandma is watching my plate, as usual. No uneaten bite gets past her; it's kind of annoying.

"I am." I scoop up a mouthful before she can jump into her food-is-nourishment lecture.

She nods, seeming satisfied.

I swallow. "Grandma?"

"Yeah, kiddo?"

"How old was I when we moved here?"

She drops her eyes to her plate. "Haven't I told you?"

"A while ago. You said I was little, but how little?"

She busies herself cutting her omelet. "You'd just turned four."

"Oh, so we moved here right when Gladder Hill opened?" I know from the founding story that Principal Gladder started this place eight years ago. And that kids had to be four or younger—just starting their "formative" years—to move here, and adults had to be a "mature" age, at least twenty-five. Which explains why there's no one older than twelve here except adults. And why my grade is the oldest in the school and also the biggest.

I do the math now in my head: Principal Gladder hasn't let any new people move in since the founding, so anyone currently younger than eight had to have been born here. And not too many have been, thanks to the two-kids-per-family limit.

But none of that answers my questions about the first four years of my life.

"Yep, you'd just made the age cutoff," Grandma says, not giving me any answers either.

I take a breath. "And where did we live before that?"

Grandma digs the side of her fork into her omelet. "Someone's asking a lot of questions today."

I shrug. "I was just wondering about my mom. When she left and all that."

Plastic thwacks wood. I flinch. Grandma has slammed her fork on the table and is glaring at me. "What did I tell you last time?"

I stiffen at her tone. She never snaps like this. "Last time?"

"Last time you brought this up."

My mind races, trying to remember. "You barely told me anything. Just that my dad was never in the picture...and my mom left when I was little. Can't I ask about her? I still don't know why she left or—"

"There's no point in thinking about it." Grandma's lips tighten as she pushes her chair back, scraping its legs against the floor. "Your mother abandoned us because she had other priorities—Superficial ones. It wasn't because of anything you or anyone else did, and that's all you need to know."

I stare at Grandma. My mom had Superficial thoughts too? Did I inherit mine from her?

She rises to her feet. "There's nothing else to say about it, so let's drop it."

"But—"

"Just drop it, okay?"

I open my mouth, question after question burning on my tongue, but Grandma has clamped her jaw shut—shut herself off from the topic.

She brings her dish to the sink and turns her back to me as she starts to scrub. I try to finish my dinner, but I've lost my appetite. At least for once Grandma isn't watching to make sure I've eaten. She does the dishes faster than seems possible and then sits in the rocking chair with her book of word search puzzles. Out of the corner of my eye, I watch her circling words, while different words circle my mind.

*She had other priorities—Superficial ones.*

I don't know if that makes me feel better or worse. On the one hand, I'm glad it wasn't something *I* did that made her abandon me. On the other hand, how could Superficiality make someone desert their own daughter?

Maybe if my mom met me now...if she got to know me...her priorities would change. She'd see that I'm just as important to her as I am to Grandma. As all the other kids in Gladder Hill are to their moms.

But that would require getting out of Gladder Hill, past security somehow—and then finding her, while having no idea where she is.

I guess my mom will have to stay just like my face: a big question mark.

I have the hardest time with eyes.

They never look right the first time I draw them—I always have to erase and redo. Maybe because everything seems to depend on them; getting the eyes wrong throws off the whole likeness, even more than getting the nose or the mouth wrong. I think it's the shape I struggle with. Or the lashes. Either way, Mr. Mackafee's eyes have been especially challenging today. I stare at my second attempt and then erase it. Clamping my own eyes shut, I try to picture his again. No use—too fuzzy. Maybe I've never looked at his eyes closely enough, or maybe it's been too long since I have.

I hide my sketchbook and go into the kitchen, where Grandma is folding laundry. She's been pretending our fight yesterday never happened, so I have too. Stubbornness

must be in our blood. I notice her grocery list on the table—
*bananas, butter, milk, eggs.*

"Want me to pick these up?" I point to the list.

Grandma raises an eyebrow. "You're *volunteering* to do
an errand?"

Maybe I shouldn't have done something so out of
character. I shrug, trying to play it off as an afterthought.
"I feel like going for a walk anyway. Just thought I'd offer."

"Well, I've hit the granddaughter jackpot." Grandma
grins. "Saves me going after my dentist appointment. The
card's there by the bread box."

I grab her credit card and an empty backpack and
then head downtown, straight to the general store. The shop
shutters are closed to keep the air-conditioning in, so I can't
see inside, but hopefully Mr. Mackafee is working today;
he and Mrs. Mackafee alternate shifts at random. The door
jingles when I open it. A few customers are browsing, and
sure enough, Mr. Mackafee is there at the till, organizing a
candy display. It only takes me a minute to find the groceries
on Grandma's list.

"Morning, Mr. Mackafee." I set my purchases on the
counter.

"Hiya, Zailey." He greets me with a smile. "Your

grandma's putting you to work, huh? I don't see any other kids doing a grocery run on a Saturday."

"I wanted to go for a walk anyway," I say as I fix my eyes on his. Ah, right—they have those lines at the corners, and his right eye always looks straight at me while the left seems to drift, looking past me...

"Ah, well, I don't blame you. It's a beau—" Mr. Mackafee stammers and coughs. "Er, a nice day out. Do you need a bag?"

I shake my head, wondering what he was about to say before he corrected himself. The strangest part is that I think Grandma has done something similar before. Wasn't it only a few weeks ago, when I was showing her a colored-pencil drawing I'd done of the view from the viewpoint? *Oh, that's beau—uh, lovely*, she said. Is it just a coincidence, or am I misremembering?

"Thatta girl. Friend of the environment." Mr. Mackafee is waiting for me to pay. I swipe the card and slip the groceries in my backpack. Mrs. Gillburn stands behind me with a basketful of stuff, so I step out of the way.

I only had a few seconds to get a good look at Mr. Mackafee, but that's all I needed—just enough time to refresh my memory. Now I can go straight home, get it down on paper, and move on to someone else.

"Hey, Zailey."

I turn to see Olive and Jill entering the store. "Oh, hey." I eye the door. I wasn't planning on an interruption.

"Did you come in to get the new UNO edition too?" Olive asks.

"There's a new edition?"

"Yeah, we heard they just got it in." She cranes her neck to look past me and points. "Ooh, there it is." I watch Olive and Jill rush toward the new-releases display table, stacked with products from this weekend's deliveries: glow-in-the-dark Rubik's Cubes; bubble gum in a new flavor; *Pop Hits Volume 8* cassettes complete with GLADDER HILL–APPROVED LYRICS stickers; and, sure enough, a pile of UNO boxes. *UNO: Deluxe Edition. Fast fun for everyone!*

Olive grabs the box on top, and she and Jill *ooh* and *aah* over it. It's probably the same game we all have at home, with the same rules, just different packaging. But I guess it's not too often we get new game shipments in, and how much else is there to get excited about around here? Though, if I were choosing, I'd go for the glow-in-the-dark Rubik's Cube.

"We're gonna play a round at my house now." Olive wiggles the box. "Want to join?"

I hesitate. It's been a while since Olive invited me

over. Maybe she's forgiven my Superficial question about shadows. I should be grateful and accept the invitation. I do miss hanging out with her—or with other kids in general.

But Jill looks less than thrilled about Olive's invitation. Did she just roll her eyes? And Olive was probably only inviting me to be polite.

And Mr. Mackafee's eyes—they're fresh in my mind. And there are still so many faces to add to my collection...

"Sorry," I hear myself say. "Have to bring these groceries home. They need to be refrigerated, so..."

"We can walk with you to drop them off." Olive smiles. "It's on the way."

"Oh, but I have to help my grandma with something too." My stomach twists with guilt at the lie.

Olive's smile falters. "Oh."

"Bummer." Jill sounds anything but disappointed.

"Well, maybe next time," Olive says.

"Yeah. Definitely." I nod with extra enthusiasm. "Let me know how you like the new edition."

We do a little dance of trying to get out of each other's way before they go to the till and I head out the door.

It's a million degrees outside, so I sweat my way home,

all the while wondering how it's come to be that I would rather spend a Saturday drawing in my room than hanging out with other kids.

No wonder I don't have a best friend anymore.

# 5

WHEN I GET HOME, I put away the groceries and read Grandma's note reminding me that she's gone to her dentist appointment. Even though I'm home alone, I go to my room and close my door to be safe. Then I get my face collection out from under the mattress, take it to my desk, and tackle Mr. Mackafee's eyes. This time, I nail them. Once I've transferred the image in my head onto the page, they finally look right.

I number the sketch and exhale. Sixty-three—I'm making progress. My stomach dances again.

I'm not sure why finishing the collection feels so important. It's not just that it can show me possibilities for my own face. I guess I also have this idea that if I can get them all in one place—if I can study all 102 faces of Gladder Hill side by side—it might help me understand some things. Like what sets each face apart from the others, when they all have the same basic parts. Is it just a matter of little things adding up, like the curve of a nose or the width of a forehead or the height of a cheekbone, that makes a person's face *that* person's face?

And with the sixty-three I've drawn, I've noticed five main face shapes: round, oval, square, pear, and heart. I don't know which one mine is, but based on my shadow and the feel of my jaw, I suspect square.

I wish I didn't care about this stuff. I know it's bad, wrong, against what we've been taught. But the problem with thoughts is they come and go as they please. I can usually stop my eyes from staring or my body from saying or writing or drawing certain things, but I can't stop a thought from entering my mind.

Which makes me wonder if other people in Gladder Hill have Superficial thoughts and I just don't know it.

I flip past Mr. Mackafee's face and decide to add Jeff Kimoto's mom because I passed her in the street earlier. To get the hard part over with, I tackle her eyes first. Once I think I've gotten them right, I move on to her eyebrows.

My pencil breaks as I draw the left one.

I've already sharpened the pencil so much that if I did it any more, there'd be no pencil left to hold. I search through my drawers for another one, but I'm all out. Grandma must have a pencil somewhere. I cover my sketchbook with school papers and then check the kitchen, but I can only find a pen next to Grandma's word search book. Pens are no good—I need the power to erase.

I hover in the doorway of Grandma's bedroom. She might have pencils at her desk. If she were here, I'd just ask her, but she won't be back for another hour probably. And it's not like she's secretive about her room—she always keeps her door open. She wouldn't mind me checking. Right?

I step into Grandma's purple paradise. Every shade of purple lives in here. The walls are violet, the carpet lavender, the bedding plum. I smile, remembering how the colors look even purpler in the winter, when the weather is just cool enough for us to open the shutters and let in some natural light. But when it's this hot outside, the air-conditioning is too precious.

I head to Grandma's wooden desk, one of the few non-purple things in here. The surface is bare except for some note cards and pens—no pencils. I open the drawers under the desk. A deck of cards, a ball of yarn, an old Rubik's Cube. More stationery, a few markers, highlighters, some tape.

I dig further, my eyes catching on a worn envelope labeled BARKBEE STUFF. I pull the envelope out. It's not sealed, so I peek at the papers inside. I pluck one from the top: a small, glossy rectangle.

In some ways, what it shows me makes sense: a brown puppy on a slope of grass, its legs kicked up in mid-gallop, its tongue hanging out, its open mouth curling wide as if it's smiling. A light-blue fence encloses the puppy and the grass, along with a swing set, a wheelbarrow, and what looks like a peach tree. A flare of sun peeks through the tree branches. A door in the fence stands open, revealing more grass and a little wooden boat, something like the one on my poster of Monet's painting *The Row Boat*. Beyond it, a stretch of grayish blue shimmers like the winding strip of river I can see from the viewpoint.

What I don't understand is how the image can be so crisp, so clear. More lifelike than any drawing or painting could be. How was it done? I rub the image with my fingers; it doesn't smudge or smear. I examine my fingertips: clean. No trace of paint or ink or pencil lead. I turn the image over.

Sierra Photography Studio, it says on the back. My heart skips a beat. I've never heard the word *photography*—I'll have to look it up later—but I'm more concerned with the first word. *Sierra*. I can still hear Grandma saying it.

*Sierra, come taste this.*

*That was the name of a dog I had.*

Is the dog in the picture the one Grandma was talking about? I guess she was telling the truth. I don't know why I feel disappointed.

But why was a studio named after the dog? She must have been a special pup.

More text sits at the bottom of the rectangle:

WWW.SIERRAPHOTOGRAPHYSTUDIO.COM

It looks strange with all those *W*s and no spaces, but it includes that name again. Sierra. I set the image on the desk and thumb through the envelope, hungry for any other information I can get.

CERTIFICATE OF LIVE BIRTH

I whip out the document, almost giving myself a paper cut. My name's at the top with my date of birth, followed by stuff I didn't know: TIME OF BIRTH: 2:07 PM... TOWN OF BIRTH: BARKBEE... Really? I was born that close by? I skim the text until my eyes freeze on two words: MOTHER'S NAME. And the first word after them. My heart leaps into my throat.

There it is, plain as day: the name Grandma spoke.

Sierra isn't a dog after all.

I plop onto the floor. My eyes race on across the paper.

IS MOTHER MARRIED? ☐ YES ☒ NO

Mother's Residence: 6 Creekside Road, Barkbee...

There are fewer fields for my father's info, but they've all been left blank. *He was never in the picture*, Grandma once said.

I reread my mom's info, tracing my fingers over her name, her address...

*Beep*. The key card reader sounds from the front door.

Panic snaps my body into action. I shove the birth certificate back inside the envelope and chuck it in the drawer before sliding it shut. Then I spot the glossy piece of paper I left on the desk—the image of the puppy in the fenced yard.

The shuffle of footsteps follows the click of the front door. I grab the picture and slip it inside my pocket before scurrying out into the hall.

Grandma rounds the corner as I approach my bedroom. "Hey, kiddo," she says. "Did you get the groceries?" She's *still* pretending our fight never happened. Two can play that game.

"Yep, I put them away."

"You're a star. How's the homework coming?"

"My pencil broke. Do you have an extra?"

She fishes in her purse and pulls one out. "Ta-da."

"Thanks."

I stroll back to my room with all the innocence of someone who's been doing their homework. But once I close the door behind me, I pull out the picture and look at it again, front and back, even though I've already committed both sides to memory. I was always told that life outside Gladder Hill is unhappy, but this picture seems full of happiness— from the smiling puppy to the sunbeam to the way the whole scene fills me with warm tingles. I want to go to this place, wherever it is.

I tuck the picture between the last pages of my face collection and hide it under the mattress.

# 6

HOTOGRAPHY...*PHOTOGRAPHY*... I RUN MY finger down the *P* section in Mr. Wallus's copy of the *Gladder Hill English Dictionary* between classes. The entries jump from *phosphorous* to *photon*. I frown. The word isn't there.

Then I remember another word I wanted to look up. The one the tour girl, Beryl, had mentioned. The problem is I only heard it spoken; I'm not sure how it's spelled. I flip through the pages, trying *cute, cyoot, kute, kyoot, quoot, queute, qute*... The dictionary lists none of them. Did Beryl mean *acute*, like the triangles we're learning about in geometry? No, that wouldn't make sense in the context. And I swear she said *cute*—one syllable. But there's no such entry.

"I hear that's a page-turner." Noah takes a seat next to me.

I eye him sidelong. I haven't seen him since I drew my accidental doodle last week. That worry comes over me again: Did he see it?

"What are you looking up?" He leans toward me, peering at the open pages.

"Nothing." I snap the book shut, although I don't know why. It's not like reading the dictionary is a crime. "Just... trying to expand my vocabulary."

"Ah, I get it." He nods. "You want to sound as smart as I do."

I snort. "You got me."

He folds his hands behind his head. "One can only aspire to be as articulate and eloquent as I."

"Right..." I feel my panic fade. He wouldn't be so friendly if he'd seen my doodle. Would he?

"Don't be jealous because I know all the fancy words," he says.

*What about* cute *and* photography? I want to ask. But then I'd have to explain where I heard those words. And what if they mean something bad and neither of us knows it, and then he repeats them to someone and gets in trouble?

I don't have a chance to ask anyway, because the loudspeaker crackles on. "Good morning, everyone." Principal Gladder's calm voice addresses the school for the daily announcements. "Please rise for the Gladder Hill pledge."

Like clockwork we all stand, our chair legs scraping against the floor as we place our hands over our hearts.

*On my honor, I will strive*

*To be kind to myself and others,*

*To focus on substance, not surface,*

*With regard to all people,*

*And to uphold the values of Gladder Hill.*

We recite the words in unison, words I've known by heart for as long as I've known the ABCs. Words I usually never think about, the same way I never think about why we say *bless you* when someone sneezes or why one plus one equals two.

There have, though, been a few times lately when I noticed my hand resting a bit lower than my heart. Or my voice dropping out during the third line of the pledge, even though my lips kept moving.

I catch that happening again now.

Hopefully, amid the chanting of the twelve other seventh graders, no one can tell.

"Now for today's announcements."

We all plop back down in our seats.

Principal Gladder clears her throat, and I draw a star on my notebook cover, preparing for the usual boring updates. "I have some good news to share," she says. "And some bad news. I'll start with the bad. Unfortunately one of our residents, Mr. Grinwold, was evicted from Gladder Hill yesterday."

Noah and I exchange glances of surprise. Murmurs skitter across the room. Everyone else seems surprised too, except Mr. Wallus; teachers must already know. And Olive and Jill are nodding and whispering to each other, as if it's not news to them either. But how do they know?

"I know this may come as a shock to many of you, but I'm afraid we had no other choice, seeing as a banned item was uncovered in his house over the weekend."

I can't believe it: Mr. Grinwold? The guy obsessed with gardening and pinwheels? If the item he had was forbidden, it must have had something to do with Superficiality. Did Mr. Grinwold have Superficial thoughts?

"Sshhh." Mr. Wallus hushes the class from his desk. "Principal Gladder is still speaking, people."

"We destroyed the item, of course," Principal Gladder's cool voice continues on the loudspeaker. "We don't know how he got it in, but smuggling will not be tolerated, so we'll be tightening our security and replacing all of our delivery workers, just in case. And this afternoon and evening, Officer

Jenkins and I and a few other teachers will be splitting up to conduct community-wide household searches. We've notified your parents and guardians..."

I stiffen in my chair. Household searches? I think of my face collection sitting under my mattress. Could it get Grandma and me evicted?

"I want to trust everyone," Principal Gladder goes on, "and I know you all know better than Mr. Grinwold. But I need to make sure everyone is cooperating with our mission. On the bright side"—her voice perks up—"this means we now have a house available, and we'll be taking a lucky family off the waiting list for the first time since we opened. They meet all our criteria for new residents, so we're excited to welcome them in a few weeks and hope you'll all be hospitable..."

Principal Gladder keeps talking, but I've stopped listening. My mind is racing through each nook and cranny of my house. How thorough will the household searches be? Maybe I should find a better place to hide my face collection. But where? I could put it at the bottom of my underwear drawer. The inspectors wouldn't check there, would they? Or maybe I can slip it in the trash bin temporarily. They wouldn't dig through the trash, would they? But then my sketchbook would get dirty and smelly. I could bury it in the backyard...

but will someone see me? And will I even get home before the searches start?

I spend the rest of the day watching the clock, even during orchestra practice, which I normally don't mind. Mrs. Pewter hands out new sheet music—another Mozart piece— but I have trouble learning it because I keep checking the time or thinking of places to hide my collection. I slide my bow along the strings of my cello so it looks like I'm trying. There are plenty of other instruments to block out my sound—six violins, two violas, one bass, and another cello—and it's not like I'm missing anything. This song won't be much different from the others we've learned. It's always Mozart or Haydn or the like. It would be nice to try other styles, but Ms. Pewter says we're limited to string-only arrangements. Something about not having "brass" instruments here—whatever those are.

When Ms. Pewter finally dismisses us, I put away my cello and rush to the door. I want to run, but I force myself to speed-walk home so I don't raise suspicion or sweat even more. The only time I slow is when I pass Mr. Grinwold's house. All his pinwheels are gone. I didn't notice on the way to school this morning because I was so focused on not being late. He really did leave, then. I wonder where he moved to, especially on such short notice. I didn't even get to say goodbye, not that we were close or anything—all we ever did was say hello in passing—but he always seemed nice. None of us at school knew him too well; he lived alone and mostly kept to himself, but he was the last person I'd suspect of Superficiality.

I continue up and over the hill, not even stopping to enjoy the viewpoint. As I turn onto my street, I spot Officer Jenkins ahead of me, coming out of the Fringle family's house, waving goodbye to Mr. Fringle. He whistles and heads on to the next house, the Scorsettis'. Mine is the one after that.

He rings the bell. I wait until Mrs. Scorsetti lets him in before I break into a sprint. When I tumble inside, I'm glad Grandma isn't in the kitchen to greet me; I can't get held up. Her wallet and key card sit on the table though. "Hi, Grandma," I call as I hurry to my room.

"Hey, kiddo," she calls back from her own room. "Did they tell you the news in school?"

"Yep. Just gonna change into clean clothes." I close my door behind me, prop my desk chair under the doorknob, and pull my collection out from under the mattress. I don't have time to bury it in the backyard or destroy it. I don't think I can bring myself to destroy it anyway.

I glance down at my bed again. I kneel and reach under

the bed, feeling for the loose floorboard. I haven't needed it in years, not since that time I hoarded lollipops because I'd gotten a cavity and Grandma said I couldn't have candy. Times sure have changed.

My fingers find the floorboard and pull it up. I drop my sketchbook into the opening, hoping it's a good enough hiding spot. Then I set the floorboard back in place and slide a shoebox over it.

Just as the doorbell rings.

# 7

THE DOORBELL RINGS AGAIN.

"Grandma?" I call. "Want me to get that?" I find her in her room rifling through one of her desk drawers, furrowing her eyebrows. She straightens at my voice.

"What are you looking for?" I ask.

"Oh, nothing." She shuts the drawer. The doorbell rings a third time. "I'll get it." She scurries past me out of the room.

I look at the closed drawer, the one where I found the picture of the puppy. Could Grandma have been looking for it? But why right now, before the house search? It doesn't seem like the sort of thing that would be considered Superficial; it's not like it depicts a human. Maybe I should put it back in her drawer before she figures out I have it...

"Come in, come in." Grandma greets Officer Jenkins. "Can I get you a drink? Tea? Juice?"

I listen from the hallway. "I'm fine, thanks, Hazel.

Been offered something at every house so far. I'm about to burst."

They both chuckle. He clears his throat. "Sorry about this, by the way. Just a formality. Shouldn't take long."

"Of course. You're just doing your job. I think it's great she's having you do this for peace of mind. Real shame about Ed though."

"Really is. Never would have thought."

"Never in a million years. What was it that he had exactly?"

"A spoon, of all things."

"A spoon? Like…"

"Yep. Plain stainless steel. Not coated or brushed or painted or anything."

I hear Grandma cluck her tongue. I have no idea what they're talking about. All of our spoons are made of recyclable plastic or silicone, aren't they?

"Apparently Joe Sutterfield was over there for lunch and a game of cards. Used the bathroom and was looking in the closet for more toilet paper. And there it was, hidden behind a box of tissues."

Joe Sutterfield? Olive's dad? No wonder she didn't look surprised in class. No wonder she looked almost…proud.

"Jeepers," Grandma says. "Well, props to Joe for reporting him."

"Absolutely. Now, don't mind me, I'm just going to take a quick look around."

"Of course, search away. Zailey's in her room, I think, so just kick her out when you get there."

I dart into my room and spread my school papers over my desk so it looks like I'm doing homework. Through my open door, I hear Officer Jenkins whistling and shuffling. Drawers and doors opening and closing.

Eventually his whistling approaches my room, and he knocks. "Hi, Zailey." He greets me with small talk, the usual grown-up questions about how school is going and which clubs and teams I'm part of now. After I give him the spiel, he coughs and asks me if I'd mind letting him look around.

"Sure, no problem." I flash him a smile as I step out of the room. I go to the bathroom just for something to do. After I wash my hands, I head back down the hall and glance through my doorway. Officer Jenkins is searching my bed, patting the comforter, pulling it back...and now lifting the mattress. My stomach twists as he peers under it. If I had left my face collection there, I'd be toast.

Maybe I still am toast.

I should go wait in the kitchen with Grandma, but now Officer Jenkins is kneeling and lifting the bed skirt, looking under the bed. I can't move. I hold my breath as he pulls out the shoebox. In the span of a second, I imagine Grandma and me being evicted, packing up all of our stuff, and being escorted to the front gates, everyone watching as we head out into the unknown...

A thought tingles, surprising me: Would it really be so bad? It would mean I don't have to wait till I'm eighteen to see what's beyond the gates.

Officer Jenkins peers inside the shoebox. I can't even remember what I have in there—shoes, I guess—but it doesn't interest him, because he slides it back under the bed before dropping the bed skirt and rising to his feet, groaning from the effort. I scurry to the kitchen before he can look up and see me.

I'm off the hook—*phew*. I won't be getting us evicted. That was a lapse of judgment I had back there: of course I don't *want* us to be evicted. This is our home. Not to mention the humiliation we'd face and Grandma's disappointment in me. The prospect of eviction should scare me, not excite me. What was I thinking?

Just another Bad Thought to add to my list.

After Officer Jenkins leaves, Grandma rolls out some whole-wheat pizza dough and makes a veggie pizza for dinner. Then we sit at the table, eating it slice by slice. "So I take it they talked to you in school about what happened with Mr. Grinwold?" Grandma says between bites.

I nod and swallow. "I was surprised. He always seemed nice."

"Yes. He did." Grandma shakes some pepper onto her pizza slice. "But people aren't always what they seem."

I fiddle with the napkin on my lap. "Doesn't it seem a little harsh though—evicting him? Just because of a spoon?"

Grandma raises an eyebrow. I guess now she knows I was eavesdropping on her and Officer Jenkins. "Well, a spoon like *that* is almost as bad as an actual mirror," she says. "Though of course you wouldn't know that. But *he* knew." Her nostrils flare. "So no, I don't think it was too harsh."

I stare at a piece of mushroom on my plate, not sure how to react. She said the M-word. It doesn't come up often. Only adults seem allowed to say it. And us kids only know it from interiority lessons and tales of the mirror demon. Even in the tales, adults never go into detail about mirrors. *As soon as the boy looked in one, the mirror demon appeared and grabbed him, pulling him through to the other side, where he was trapped forever in the cold and darkness, yadda, yadda, yadda....* I'm old enough now to know it's just a story, but it used to scare me, even though I didn't—and still don't—know what a demon or a mirror is supposed to look like. I've heard rumors, like how a mirror shows a clear image of the person looking at it and even imitates their motions. But all I know for sure is that mirrors are related to *reflections*, another word we heard in interiority lessons and then once in physics class. And reflections have to do with rays of light bouncing back from a surface.

That's how we see anything, Mr. Huttle told us last year: if you see a bird, it's because light has reflected off that bird. But certain surfaces...well, Mr. Huttle kind of rushed through this part, mumbling that we don't have to worry about it in Gladder Hill, but certain smooth and shiny surfaces reflect light in a way that shows images of things nearby.

*Things*, he said. But *things* could include people, couldn't it? Like in that mirror rumor...

"Is something wrong with the pizza?" Grandma frowns. "You've barely touched your second slice."

I swear she always has one eye on my plate. "No, it's great," I say, lifting my slice to take another bite. She nods and smiles.

I chew and swallow. "I was just wondering..." My heart starts to pump faster. "Have you ever looked at one?" The question tumbles out of me before I can change my mind.

"Looked at what?" Grandma puts another slice on her plate.

"You know..."

She glances up and blinks. I may have made a huge mistake. This might be worse than asking about my mom—the other M-word.

But *she's* the one who brought up *this* M-word.

I wait, bracing myself for a scolding.

She breathes in through her nose. "Yes," she says, to my surprise. "Before Gladder Hill. And that's how long it's been since I've..." She turns her gaze to the kitchen window, even though the shutters are closed. "I'm grateful, you know. I was younger then..." The lines around her mouth and eyes deepen. I try to imagine Grandma as a younger woman, even a kid like me. I try to imagine her without those lines. I can't.

"Why would we want to watch ourselves grow old?" she murmurs. I stare at her, not knowing what to say—and not even sure she's talking to me. She squints into space. Is this why she isn't bothered to try contact lenses? It occurs to me now that maybe she doesn't mind going blind.

Blindness would be more effective than any ban or rule in Gladder Hill.

Grandma blinks again and pulls her eyes back to me, clearing her throat. Adjusting her place mat. "What I mean is you're lucky to grow up here. That's all you need to know. Gladder Hill's the kindest place we could live nowadays."

I have no point of comparison, but from the way Grandma says it, I can tell she believes it with her whole heart.

And maybe I should too.

*Everyone's gladder in Gladder Hill.* I guess Grandma's right that I'm lucky: as the founding story goes, Principal Gladder received hundreds of applications but could only take about a hundred residents, and I was one of them. Granted, I only had to meet one criterion: age. Adults had to also be able to fill one of the job or volunteer roles and, of course, demonstrate their commitment to Gladder Hill's mission. When you're four or younger, I guess other people choose your mission—your beliefs—for you.

"And," Grandma says, resuming her casual tone as she pushes back her chair and stands, "a new family will be moving in soon. That's exciting."

I've been so busy processing what happened with Mr. Grinwold that I haven't given much thought to the new people. New faces. I guess Grandma's right—that part *will* be exciting. "I wonder if they'll like pinwheels too," I say.

Grandma laughs and carries her plate to the sink.

As I collect the other dishes and put them in the dishwasher, Grandma says, "Oh, could you make sure your floor is clear of stuff before you go to bed? I'm vacuuming the house tomorrow."

"Why?"

She laughs again. "Have you seen the floors, kiddo? A cleaning day's overdue. I realized it when Officer Jenkins was here. Bit embarrassing."

I try not to panic as I load the dishwasher. I managed to get through the last couple of months and even today's house search without being discovered, but Grandma's cleaning day means she'll be focusing on my floor. Even if I put my face collection back under the mattress, she'll still be in my room, poking around. And it's been a few months since she flipped our mattresses; she could do that any day now.

I turn on the dishwasher and go back into my room, closing the door and propping the chair under the doorknob again. Then I take out my collection and search for another, better hiding spot. If I could hide it in the walls, I would, but there's no way to do that. No place in here seems safer than under the floorboard.

I sigh and open the sketchbook since I already have it out. I take it to my desk. I don't realize who I'm about to draw until my pencil meets the paper.

Mr. Grinwold begins to materialize; somehow I hadn't drawn him yet. And now he's time-sensitive. I'll never be able to look at him again, to get a visual refresher, even though I got one almost every day on my walks to and from school. Luckily I can still see him: his shy smile, his huge nostrils, the receding front edge of his hair. I can hear his voice too. "Howdy," he'd call, or, "Mornin'," or sometimes he'd say nothing at all and just wave—even salute on occasion. Though I never got to know him, I always thought of him as friendly.

This is what happens when I draw faces. With each stroke, I find myself thinking about interactions I've had with that person. Moments. I feel as though I'm getting to know my subject better. I find myself thinking: What kind of person are they? Nice, mean, shy, sarcastic? And how can I get that across in my sketch? I want it to have some impression of their personality, their spirit...not just their face. Mr. Grinwold was always jovial, so I add a twinkle to his eye.

Once I finish him, I stretch my arms and number today's

addition: seventy-five. Butterflies flutter in my stomach. At this rate I could finish the collection in a couple of weeks. Maybe less.

As long as Grandma doesn't find it first.

And with her plans to vacuum the floors tomorrow, there's nothing else for it: I'll have to bring the face collection with me to school.

It will be safer in my locker anyway. At least there I can lock it up.

# 8

THE ONE THING I know about my face is how it feels.

My fingertips have met the same terrain and textures for years. Smooth here, rougher there. Fine hairs here, a curve there, a dip here.

But this morning, as I brush my teeth and reach up to scratch an itch, my fingers bump into something unfamiliar. They bump into a bump.

I prod my chin. The bump is smaller than my fingertip, and hard.

I spit out my toothpaste and drop my toothbrush in its holder. Then I rub my hands all over my face. But I don't feel any other bumps like it. I turn on the sink, gather the cloudy water in my cupped hands, and then splash it on my chin to see if the bump is something that can wash off.

I pat my chin dry and still feel it there.

"Zailey?" Grandma calls from the hall. "It's seven thirty, kiddo."

Seven thirty? I'll be late for school if I don't leave soon. "Almost ready," I call as I hurry out of the bathroom and into my room. I yank open my dresser drawers. Luckily I don't have much of a decision to make clothes-wise. On another day I might give some thought to what color T-shirt or pants I feel like wearing, since color is the only difference between them, but today I just grab one of each at random. I tie the drawstring on my pants and pull the shirt over my head. It still fits loosely like it's supposed to, but it protrudes a little in the chest area.

My cheeks go hot, remembering the talk Dr. Daya gave me at my last doctor's appointment. About how kids around my age start to experience changes in their bodies. Changes that mean you're growing from a kid into an adult. At first I couldn't believe she was talking about my body, but then I remembered it's okay if it's for medical reasons. She said every seventh grader was getting the talk. I glance again at the two bumps in my T-shirt and then feel the one on my chin. Dr. Daya didn't mention face bumps, but lately I've noticed some red ones on other kids' faces—Malorie Windleson's and Jeff Kimoto's—so maybe mine is like theirs. Or maybe—

"Zailey?"

I drop my hand. "Coming!" I seize my backpack and dart down the hall.

"Did someone oversleep?" Grandma is eating yogurt in the kitchen.

"Just some last-minute studying," I lie. The irony is that's what I should have been doing. I stayed up late working on my face collection and fell asleep before I could study: a first for me. At least I got to add some new faces. Mr. and Mrs. Stellings, their two kids, the chiropractor...

"You'll have to eat on the way." Grandma gets up and hands me a banana and a granola bar. I nod and hold my breath, waiting for some flicker in her eyes or shift in her expression as she notices whatever the bump on my chin is. But she just kisses me on the forehead and sits back down. Maybe it's nothing after all.

Then again, Grandma is always careful about where she looks. Most people in Gladder Hill are.

I clutch my bag to my chest as I walk into school. It feels heavy with eighty faces inside. I tuck the collection at the back of my locker. It looks like any small notebook, really—it could be full of boring school notes. Still, I make sure to bury it behind books and folders. Then I shut my locker door and turn the dial till it clicks.

Is it extra hot in the hallway today, or is it just me?

I check an AC vent on my way to class, but cool air blows onto my hand as usual. Just me, then.

As we wait for class to start, everyone's talking about yesterday's house searches—probably because it's the most exciting thing to happen here in maybe forever. I think some kids are hoping for more drama, another eviction. But after Principal Gladder's voice crackles through the loudspeaker for the Gladder Hill pledge, she says she's pleased to inform us that no inappropriate items were found yesterday. Most of us lose interest after that. The rest of the morning announcements concern boring things: a rescheduling of the annual spelling bee, a reminder that it's hair trim day for grades six and seven, and an update on the community college initiative.

"I know a lot of your parents have been asking for this," Principal Gladder says now. "So I'm glad to announce we secured the funding to establish Gladder Hill College. That will involve adding a new wing to this building, which we'll be working on over the next several years. It should be ready in time for our oldest students, our current seventh graders. Admissions will, of course, only be open to Gladder Hill residents, and full scholarships will be available for all incoming students. I'm delighted you'll all have this option when the time comes…"

I draw stars on my notebook cover and try not to roll my eyes. We're not even done with seventh grade, and the adults are already trying to convince us to stay in Gladder Hill when we grow up. Just in case their claims about life outside the gates—how unhappy it is—aren't enough. But are those claims really true? The picture I found in Grandma's room gives me a happy feeling, and Beryl mentioned pep rallies that are "super fun." I'm not sure what a pep rally is, but the last time I checked, fun makes people happy.

Well, once I turn eighteen, I'll be a legal adult, and no one will be able to stop me from leaving if I want to.

I wonder if I'll still want to—if I'll have the guts. Exciting as it seems, the idea scares me too.

Mr. Wallus begins class with a boring lecture on Latin root words. I start to take notes, but as always, the notes turn into doodles: stars and flowers and random squiggles. This time, I make sure they don't become more than that. Still, my staring problem seems to have gotten worse—even in this classroom where the desk setup makes it harder to see faces. If Mr. Wallus could do me a favor and make his lectures interesting for once, maybe my eyes wouldn't wander the room, trying to sneak peeks of my classmates. I tell myself it's just for research purposes—I'm observing for the collection. *Observing* sounds nicer than *staring*.

But maybe, just maybe, I'm also looking for hints. Could my bump look something like the raised brown spot above Jen Rosenthal's left eyebrow? But she's always had that, and my bump is new. Malorie Windleson had a red dot on her nose the other day, and now it's gone, while three new ones form a triangle on her forehead. Sort of like the cluster that keeps growing on Jeff Kimoto's chin. Could mine be like *those* bumps?

But no matter how long I stare, I don't—and won't—get any closer to knowing.

And I don't care about not knowing, I remind myself yet again. Life is full of mysteries, like death and outer space, and my face is just another on the list.

*Don't you have the right to know?* Beryl's voice echoes in my head.

I look down at my hands, my arms, my legs, my feet... I know them well. But not my face. It's mine, and yet everyone in Gladder Hill has seen it except me.

The more I think about it, the more I wonder if Beryl was right: *it doesn't seem fair.*

The best thing about trim day is that it takes up class time.

"All right, Zailey, have a seat." Mr. Hollins waves me over to the barber chair as Jen Rosenthal rises from it with a newly buzzed head.

Granted, it's only five minutes of class time, but that's better than nothing. And Mr. Hollins always lets each of us take a piece of candy from his Buzz Bowl. I grab a Jolly Rancher before I drop into the chair.

He clips the cape around me. "How are things, hun?"

"Not bad," I say, wondering if he'll look at my chin— if he'll react at all to whatever new sight exists there. But he just swivels the chair around so I'm facing the wall.

"But not good?" He turns on the electric clipper, and I can feel its ceramic blades start to glide up the back of my skull.

I laugh. "Just boring, I guess. You must get bored doing this all day too?"

"Nah. I get to chat with you kids. Now tilt your head forward for me, okay?"

I know the drill. As I tip my head, some hair clippings slide down the front of my cape and onto the floor, joining other short hairs in an array of colors: dark hairs mixed with lighter ones, yellowish and some orange; the orange must be Malorie Windleson's. All together like that, they form a mass that makes me think of the tour girl Beryl's hair, the bulk of waves reaching her shoulders. I pick a few fallen hairs off my lap: black, like the hairs on my arms and legs. And short like them too. I wonder what it feels like to have all those longer strands hanging around your face and over your ears and neck. Maybe Beryl would have told me if I'd asked her...

"You okay, hun?" Mr. Hollins pauses the clippers. "Did I nick you?"

I must have been fidgeting. "No, sorry, just a little hot."

"Even with the AC? I can turn it up..."

"No, it's okay, the trim's helping." It's true; I already feel a little cooler as he buzzes more hair off the top of my head.

Mr. Hollins chuckles. "A bonus for sure. Even half an inch off makes a difference in this heat."

A bonus—right. I always think of the heat as the main reason we keep our heads shaved, but I guess it has more to do with why we all wear the same type of loose T-shirts and pants. To *minimize physical comparison*—a phrase Principal Gladder threw around a lot in interiority lessons. Not that our clothing has stopped me from noticing how arms and legs and middles are, like heads, different shapes and sizes. Some are wider, some narrower, some longer, some shorter...

And maybe the buzz cuts are supposed to stop me from noticing hair differences, but if that's the goal, why don't they shave the hair on our arms too? I seem to have more than most kids, or at least most girls. Even more than Mr. Hollins, I think. I peek at his arms as he reaches for the neck duster on the counter. His hairs are lighter, so it's harder to tell how much there is. His skin is lighter too, but I'm still puzzling out how hair and skin are connected. Lighter hair usually goes with lighter skin, but darker hair doesn't always go with darker skin. Neither does thicker hair. Take Olive, for instance: her hair seems as dark as my arm hair, but her skin looks lighter. Is there any rhyme or reason to all this?

"All right, Zailey." Mr. Hollins interrupts my Superficial thoughts. "You're all set." He brushes hair clippings off my neck and shoulders and removes the cape, just as Olive walks in for her turn. Her last name comes right after mine in the alphabet, so she always goes next. My chest pangs as I remember that's how we became friends in the first place.

"Be right with you, hun," Mr. Hollins says to Olive. "Quick bathroom break."

Olive gives him a thumbs-up and takes a Tootsie Pop from the Buzz Bowl.

I make a point of smiling as I get up from the barber seat. "How was UNO Deluxe? I meant to ask."

Olive laughs. "Basically the same as regular UNO." She plops into the chair and unwraps her Tootsie Pop. "Are you doing anything after school today?"

I hesitate. Today's one of those rare afternoons when I have no activities—no orchestra practice, no Rubik's Cube club, no Frisbee matches. And Olive knows that because she does all the same things.

She goes on before I can answer. "Me and Jill and a few others are gonna play a round at Wonderland. You've *got* to come." She licks the Tootsie Pop. "We need someone to beat Ricky for once. Keep his ego in check."

*For once.* They must play mini golf together a lot. "I don't have any money with me," I say, which is true.

"Kids play free the first of the month, remember? And I'll buy you an ice cream after. Come on, how can you say no to that?" She wiggles her eyebrows and grins.

I can't tell if this is a pity invite again or if she actually wants me to come, but her smile makes it hard to say no—the way it brightens her eyes, lifts her cheeks, and makes her face look heart-shaped. And I should go while I still, just barely, have friends to play mini golf with. It would be a normal thing to do, unlike drawing faces in my room.

"Okay." I nod and try to sound excited. "Count me in."

# 9

THE WONDERLAND MINI GOLF Course is as exotic as it gets in Gladder Hill. At least, it's the closest you can come to feeling like you're somewhere else. Sure, the life-size structures are a bit random—the dragon, the castle, the dinosaur, the windmill, the giant octopus... But they give you this sense of having traveled somewhere. Even though it's a one-minute walk from school.

That's why, despite my reluctance at the barber, a tingle of excitement spreads through me as I approach the entrance: the big archway with its castle-like turrets and fake climbing vines and giant red-and-white mushrooms. Wonderland is one of those places that will probably never lose its magic.

Olive and the others are waiting out front: Jill, Hal Gotwell, and Ricky Sanchez. They're all laughing about something and don't see me yet; my pace wavers, as does my excitement. I force myself to keep walking until I'm standing a foot away.

They still don't notice me, so I clear my throat. "Hey." Why do I feel like an intruder? I have to remind myself that Olive invited me.

Olive looks up. "Oh, yay, there you are."

"Hey," the others say in unison. Did Jill just glance at my chin, or did I imagine it? I resist the urge to reach up and check if the bump is still there. I haven't checked in at least an hour.

As we head into Wonderland, a few younger kids already stand in line at the front desk. The sun beats down, so I pull my sun visor out of my bag and Velcro it on. I'm glad I decided to leave my face collection in my locker. Taking it with me seemed risky. It could fall out of my bag, or I could set my bag down somewhere and lose track of it... Better to avoid those possibilities.

"Man, I'm already melting." Olive lifts her sun visor and wipes her forehead. "It's like we're on the surface of the sun."

"We basically are." Hal snorts. "When was the last time it rained?"

"At least two months ago," I say, feeling the need to contribute something. "And even then, it wasn't much." I remember how the little rain that fell got soaked up by the dirt roads or disappeared into the hundreds of drain holes covering Gladder Hill. It happened during a school day too, so we couldn't even go out and dance in it.

"Well, that's why Principal Gladder picked this part of America, isn't it?" Jill says with a know-it-all air. "Less rain."

I squint at her. "How do you know that?"

"I overheard my mom telling my dad."

"But what does she have against rain?" Olive frowns.

Jill shrugs. "Maybe she hates getting wet."

Of course—Jill doesn't actually know more than we do. She just wants us to think she does.

We get our golf clubs, balls, and scorecards from Ms. Koy at the front desk and head to the first hole: the pink elephant. Hal goes first; his ball rolls under the elephant's legs and comes to a stop a foot away from the hole.

"Ooh, close one," Olive says.

Mini golf is one of those situations where it's acceptable to stare at someone, at least while they're playing. That means I get a refresher on Hal and Jill, whose faces I haven't drawn yet. But that also means they're all looking at me when my turn comes. It makes it a little hard to concentrate. I can feel everyone watching me, even as they keep chatting. And I find myself turning my head so they can't see my chin. My shadow on the fake grass distracts me. I tap the ball too hard, and it hits the elephant's leg. Instead of going underneath, it bounces up and off the elephant's butt and then back toward me.

"It's okay, we're just warming up." Olive smiles.

As we move through the rest of the course, I force myself to concentrate more. It turns out Olive was right—I just needed to warm up—because I end up getting a hole in one at the fourth hole, the giant spider and web.

"Niiice," Hal bellows. Olive whoops. Ricky huffs, his high score threatened.

I don't do quite as well on the next few holes, but I still get the ball in on the second putt. I'm feeling good by the last hole, the dragon, and I don't know if it's because I'm playing well or because I feel like part of the group and am actually having fun—but either way, the afternoon is going a lot better than I expected.

I get another hole in one to end the game, and even though Ricky wins, second place isn't half bad.

We return our clubs and golf balls, laughing about Hal's grumpiness: he's not happy he came in last. "Ice cream'll make you forget," Ricky says, elbowing Hal as we head to the ice cream stand. You can't play mini golf at Wonderland without getting ice cream after; it's tradition. Some people even come just for the ice cream, but it tastes more satisfying after a game of mini golf. And anyone with a score of fifteen putts or fewer gets a free scoop.

"I can't believe she's building a college but not a skate park," Ricky says to Olive as we wait in line.

"Or a new obstacle course," Olive says. "I've done the one at the adventure center a hundred times."

"I'm just saying, we could use a skate park *now*. It'll be years till we use the college."

I adjust my visor. "Are you guys all gonna go to college here?" I try to sound casual.

"Yeah, why not?" Ricky says. "It'll be right here."

Hal shrugs. "My parents think it's a good idea. Won't put us in debt like other colleges, apparently."

"And it will be a *top* college." Jill fans herself. "With jobs lined up for all of us."

"What jobs?" I ask.

"Didn't you read the thing they handed out the other day?" She reaches into her bag and pulls out the college brochure I'd tucked in a folder to read later. The third page is titled CAREERS IN GLADDER HILL and explains how there will be enough job openings for every kid who wants one when we grow up—that's why parents aren't allowed to have more than two kids—plus plenty of volunteer opportunities, so no one will ever be bored.

Page four is filled with a long list of job titles. *Physician (2), paramedic (1), nurse (2), dentist (1), eye doctor (1), pharmacist (1), librarian (1)...* They're basically all the jobs the adults have now—all the jobs Principal Gladder needed to fill when she founded Gladder Hill. The only one that interests me is art teacher, but the art teacher has to teach at least one other subject, like Mr. Huttle does. I don't mind English and math...but would I like teaching them? I guess Gladder Hill doesn't need to employ an artist, and even if it did, I wouldn't be able to draw the things I'm most interested in...

"I think I'm gonna go for the veterinarian slot," Jill says. "I can play with cats all day."

"Oh, I was gonna go for that." Olive laughs. "Awkward."

"Maybe there are more veterinarian jobs outside Gladder Hill," I murmur.

Olive, Jill, Ricky, and Hal all turn and stare at me. Is the idea really that scandalous?

"Well, there are plenty of other jobs here." Jill points at the list. "Why would we leave? Everything's better here."

"Yeah, everyone's gladder in Gladder Hill, remember?"

Olive says. "It makes no sense to go somewhere we won't be as happy."

"Right." I pretend to adjust my visor again. They all seem to believe it—to be content with the idea of never setting foot outside the gates. I start to feel like I did at the entrance to Wonderland: an intruder in the group. The odd one out.

Olive glances sidelong at me. "*You* don't want to leave, do you, Zailey?"

"No," I lie, holding my breath. The sun beats down harder than ever.

She smiles. "Good."

I exhale. I think she believes me—or maybe she just wants to. She wants to believe that the Zailey who once asked her about shadows has come to her senses. That my Superficial streak has passed and she doesn't have to worry anymore that I might infect her with my Bad Thoughts.

"Sucks for Mr. Grinwold though," Ricky says. "He can never come back."

Jill shrugs. "Serves him right."

"Do you really think he deserved to be evicted?" I say, knowing I should hold my tongue. But I can't help it.

Olive whirls on me. "Of course he deserved it. He had

a banned item. And was obviously using it for Superficial reasons." She raises an eyebrow. "You think he didn't deserve it?"

"I didn't say that."

I can feel the other three watching us. Olive stares at me like she doesn't know what to make of me, and I try to hold her gaze. That is, until Mr. Reed calls, "Next."

She looks away first and moves up to the counter, ordering her ice cream from Mr. Reed and leaving me with a chill up my back. I watch her order and realize that if she found my drawings, she would probably do just as her dad did to Mr. Grinwold. She wouldn't hesitate to tell on me. Once again I'm glad I left the collection in my locker.

Ice cream, at least, is a delicious distraction. I show Mr. Reed my scorecard and order my favorite: a scoop of mint chocolate chip on a sugar cone. I take a lick and relish it. Ice cream may not be at the top of the Nourish & Flourish food pyramid, but nothing compares. Besides, the pyramid encourages us to include food we enjoy in our day, as long as we balance stuff from the top and the bottom; I'm sure whatever Grandma cooks for dinner will even it out.

And it's always a nice break to eat something without Grandma watching. Without her gaze checking my progress.

Without her questions: Why haven't I touched this or finished that?

I take another lick and realize, with a rush of guilt, that I enjoy eating more when Grandma's not around.

We look for a picnic table, but they're all taken. Olive points out one with only three people, leaving enough room for the five of us. As we head toward it, I realize the three people are Noah and his friends Tony and Jen.

"Can we join you guys?" Ricky asks.

"I guess we can put up with you." Tony slides over, and so do Noah and Jen on the other side.

I end up across from Noah. As the others fall into conversation, Noah points at my ice cream. "Better pick up the pace," he says.

I look down to find mint-green streaks dripping down the side of the cone onto my hand. "I'm never fast enough," I groan, taking another lick.

"It's like a race against the sun."

The only trace of Noah's ice cream is a pink smudge on his chin. "And you won," I say. "What flavor did you get? Strawberry?"

"How'd you know?"

"Lucky guess. Any good?"

"Out of this world. And maybe even this universe."

"Wow. Are you still into that stuff? Space and all that?" I remember when he became obsessed with astronomy a couple of years ago after we learned a little about the solar system. There wasn't much to go on besides a short chapter in our textbook, but Noah decorated his locker with cut-outs of the planets.

He grins. "I mean, I don't play Space Race five times a day anymore, just twice. But yeah, I still think it would be cool to be an astronomer."

"So do you want to go up into space someday?" I take off my visor and wipe sweat from my forehead. It's too hot to put it back on, so I leave it on the table.

"Nah, too freaky. I just like reading about it all." He stretches his arms above his head. "Besides, I should probably see more of *this* planet before I explore others."

My tongue pauses mid-lick. Does that mean he wants to leave Gladder Hill? I realize astronomer wasn't one of the jobs listed on the college brochure. Does he want to go to college somewhere else too? I'm itching to ask, but Olive is sitting right next to me, chatting with Jill and Tony, and she might hear.

"Yeah, it's kind of funny how little we know about our

own planet," is all I dare to say. He laughs and looks like he's about to say something else, but then someone pulls out an UNO deck, ending our conversation.

We play a round of UNO with sticky fingers, laughing when Tony gets the hiccups. After Ricky wins, Olive and Jill say they need to head home. I get up too, explaining that I have to run back to the school for a book I forgot—which is partly true. We say bye to the others, and at the Wonderland exit— another archway with fake climbing vines and the words HAVE A WONDERful day—I tell Olive and Jill I'll see them tomorrow.

The school's a minute away, and though all the heat and sun has made me sluggish, I find myself smiling as I walk up to the front doors. The afternoon wasn't so bad. Maybe I'm not friendless after all.

Inside, a few people still roam the halls: kids getting out of club meetings or practices that ran late. I guess I could have gone straight home; what's one night without working on my collection? But I just got a refresher on some faces at Wonderland, and I don't want to waste it. So I head to my locker, taking a moment to "itch" my chin for the first time in hours; the bump is still there, and it feels bigger than before. Somehow I forgot about it after the first hole at Wonderland; I miss that blissful unawareness.

I sigh and rummage in my locker, pulling out my face collection.

"Yo, Zailey! You forgot this."

I jump at Noah's voice; my sketchbook slips from my grip. For a split second, my eyes can't decide what to follow—the voice or the sketchbook. In the end they go for the sketchbook, plunging to where it has fallen open at my feet.

Open and not facedown.

Jill and Mr. Mackafee stare up at me from two opposite pages. I dive and snatch up my collection. "You caught me off guard," I squeak, trying not to panic as I snap the sketchbook shut and shove it in my backpack. Maybe Noah didn't have time to see.

But when I look up and find him a few feet away, clutching my sun visor, his Pop Eyes are fixed on the spot on the floor where my collection was just lying.

And I know my secret is no longer a secret.

# 10

NOAH LIFTS HIS GAZE from the floor and gapes at me. "I knew it," he sputters. "Ever since I saw your doodle in class..."

So he did see it that time. I've been careless, so careless.

"How'd you learn to do that?" He looks at the floor again, as if the sketchbook is still lying there. "I mean, they seemed so... Jill, and Mr. Mackafee, they seemed so..."

His words surprise me—and fill me with strange pride. He could tell who they were? They weren't labeled or anything.

Then I remember where we are. I glance over my shoulder, down the empty hall. Even though we seem to be alone, we're still at school. Anyone could be around. "We shouldn't talk here," I say. "Are you walking home now?"

"Well, I was about to, but—"

"Come on. Oh, and I'll take that." I point at my visor still in his hand. He passes it to me with a dazed look, and

I usher him outside onto Main Street. I walk fast, and I can see Noah in my periphery trying to keep up. He follows me along Mojave Lane, past a dozen houses including his own, and then I veer off, leading him up the hill until we finally crest it and reach the viewpoint.

I stop and turn to him. "You're not going to tell Principal Gladder, are you?" I half whisper, even though we're well away from other people.

Noah rubs the back of his neck. Ice cream still streaks his chin. "Well, technically I should…"

My panic rises. "I'll give you my allowance. My lunch for a week. My Space Race cards." I know I'm begging now, but what choice do I have?

"I already have a deck."

"What about my scooter? I barely use it."

"I prefer my skateboard."

"You can have my Boggle set—a special edition. Or I'll do your homework for a month. Anything."

"Anything?"

I narrow my eyes. "Within reason."

He licks his lips and runs a hand over the top of his buzz cut. "All right." He lowers his voice. "Let me see mine, and I won't tell."

"Your what?"

His ears redden. He points at my bag. "Aren't I in there too?"

"Wait..." I blink as it hits me what he's saying.

Shock—or maybe relief—floods me so fast that I can't help it: a laugh escapes me.

Noah's cheeks match his ears in color now, and his jaw tightens. "Okay, then. I'll go find Principal Gladder. Makes no difference to me." He starts to turn.

"No." I grab his arm. "Okay. Fine. Okay." I take a breath. "I haven't gotten to you yet, but I can add you tonight and show it to you tomorrow. Somewhere secret. All right?"

"All right. And you have to let me keep it."

"What?" I step back. "No way."

"Why not?"

"You said to let you *see* it."

"What's the difference?"

"A huge difference. If I let you keep it, you could show someone. Or use it to get me in trouble." My voice wavers. "Get my grandma and me evicted."

"I wouldn't do that."

"How can I be sure?"

"I promise. Cross my heart or pinky swear or whatever

you want me to do." Noah's gaze and voice don't falter, but I'm still not convinced.

Suddenly I remember a fancy term Mr. Huttle mentioned during art class once. "Well, I own all rights to my work," I say. "By default. Remember what we learned about intelligent property?"

"You mean *intellectual* property?" The corner of Noah's mouth twitches.

"Whatever, close enough."

Noah thinks for a moment, chewing the inside of his cheek. "Okay, then I'll buy it from you."

"Like, with money?"

"That's usually how people buy things."

His sarcasm, ironically, makes me realize he's serious. And it dawns on me: I could get *paid* for my art. That's what makes someone a professional artist, isn't it? Mr. Huttle said Monet sold his first artwork when he was fifteen, so this would give me an almost three-year lead. How cool would that be?

But doubt comes next. "Do you even have any money?" I ask him. Generally, twelve-year-olds don't have much. My monthly allowance is a dollar.

"I can give you two bucks for it," Noah says.

I snort. "That's barely enough for a candy bar."

"Fine, three bucks. Unless there's something else you want instead?"

I hesitate. *Is* there something else I want?

I scratch my chin; my finger bumps into the bump. Noah's gaze hasn't fallen there—that I've noticed anyway—but the bump feels bigger than ever.

"We could do a trade." The words slip out of me.

"What do you mean, a trade?"

"A drawing for a drawing." Am I really saying this?

There go his Pop Eyes again. "You want *me* to draw *you*?"

"Sshh." I look around, feeling ridiculous now. Ashamed. Even though *he* asked the same thing of me.

He shrugs. "All right."

Butterflies come to life in my stomach.

"But I can't draw too well," he adds.

The butterflies pause. I hadn't considered that. I think of his sunrise in art class—the M-shaped birds. "I can give you lessons," I say.

He brightens. "Really?"

"Sure," I squeak, feeling anything but sure.

"Maybe this will help me get a better grade in art class too."

I'm afraid to ask what his current grade is.

"Wanna do the first lesson now?" Noah sits in the brown grass and looks up at me expectantly.

"Here?" The butterflies resume, fluttering around the pit of my stomach. "We should do it somewhere more secret."

"Like where?"

I glance toward the low sun. "It's too late today, but can you come to my house on Friday? Right after orchestra practice? My grandma works again that day and doesn't get home till around four thirty."

"Sure." Noah wipes the back of his neck. "Kind of hot up here anyway." He squints out into the distance. "But not a bad view."

I follow his gaze to the horizon. "Yeah, it's nice, isn't it? More than nice. It's…it's…"

"Cool?" Noah offers. "Amazing? Stunning?"

"Well, it *is* all those things. But they never feel like the right word. Only I can't think of a better one. Know what I mean?"

"Actually, yeah. That's happened to me before. Like when I look at the sunrise."

"Maybe the right word doesn't exist."

"Or maybe we'll learn it in our next vocab quiz." Noah crosses his fingers.

I laugh. "Either way, this is my favorite spot in Gladder Hill."

"I need to come up here more often."

I keep my eyes ahead, but my fists clench a little. This is supposed to be *my* spot.

Then again, my secret was supposed to be my secret. And now he knows about it. More than that, he wants to be a part of it.

And I don't know how to feel about that.

"It's weird to finally talk about this stuff," he says after a minute. "Weird, but good. I thought it was just me."

My fists loosen. "Yeah. I thought I was a bad seed or something."

Noah grins. "You probably are. Just not the only one. There's at least two of us. Maybe three, if Mr. Grinwold counts."

"Aw, Mr. Grinwold. He always seemed nice."

"Wonder where he is now."

"Somewhere out there, I guess." I gesture at the horizon.

Noah pulls up some weeds by his feet. "So when did *you* start having bad-seed thoughts?"

I lean forward on my elbows; the sun casts a shape on the ground beside me. "I can't remember for sure. But I've been curious about my shadow for a while."

He perks up. "You too? Do you do that thing where you try to look at it from the side, but then it hurts to turn your head that far?"

I nod vigorously. "There was this one time I was doing that on my way to school. I tripped and fell into Ms. Hanselman's precious marigolds. Totally smushed 'em."

"No way."

"I heard her front door opening and ran."

We crack up. Noah keels over, and I clutch my stomach. It isn't even that funny, but maybe it's less to do with funniness than with something else—a feeling of release—relief.

Eventually we calm down. I wipe water from my eyes. "I should go. My grandma's expecting me home."

"Yeah, my parents too."

I adjust my backpack on my shoulder. "So...Friday after school?"

Noah nods. "And do you want to hang out tomorrow too maybe? We could meet here."

"Sure."

We exchange nervous smiles, our bad-seed plans planted and growing.

Then we part ways.

# 11

M Y PROGRESS REPORT ARRIVED today.

If I'd gotten home sooner—if I hadn't spent so long at the viewpoint with Noah—I might have seen it before Grandma did. I could have hidden it or at least braced myself for this lecture.

"You had all As and Bs last year," Grandma says. "What happened?"

I shrug and look at my hands.

"You can't neglect your studies, Zailey."

Her accusation makes me frown across the kitchen table at the report. Two As, a bunch of Bs, and one C. "It's not like I'm failing," I say.

"Not yet. You're letting your grades slip. From now on I want you to do your homework out here, at the kitchen table, where I can make sure you're doing it. Okay?"

I slump in my seat. This new rule is going to cut into my

drawing time. "Are they this hard on kids outside of Gladder Hill?" I grumble.

Grandma crosses her arms. "Are you being ungrateful?"

"No." I realize my mistake. She'll go off on a whole other lecture now.

"You should be proud. Kids outside Gladder Hill don't belong to such an intellectual community."

"Right, right, sorry." Here she goes.

"Principal Gladder has done us worlds of good, prioritizing our minds, our interiors. Saving us from the mirror demon."

I roll my eyes. "That's a children's story."

"Well, it's still a reminder of how much better off we are."

I fidget. *We.* Grandma is speaking for all of Gladder Hill, not knowing she shouldn't include me. Not knowing I'm a Gladder Hill failure. A disgrace.

Maybe it's not too late to reel myself back to the good side. There's still time to call off my plans with Noah. We only made them a half hour ago. I could tell him tomorrow, first thing...

But what about the stuff the tour girl said? *It doesn't seem fair. Don't you have the right to know?* I know now that my Superficial thoughts might not be totally out there. Noah has them too, and apparently so does Mr. Grinwold.

Still, the guilt gnaws at me for the rest of the evening—as I do my homework, as I eat dinner, as I clean dishes. Even as I sit in my room adding faces to my collection.

Even as I turn out the light and pull the bedcovers over me.

But that's when the butterflies come back too.

So much has happened today that I should fall right to sleep—I should conk out. But my mind won't turn off. I replay the whole conversation with Noah. Is he really going to draw me?

If he follows through, I'll need to take his drawing with a grain of salt. Even after I give him lessons, his drawing won't be 100 percent accurate. Even my drawings could never look exactly like the real thing.

But still, Noah's drawing will have *some* semblance of reality. My heart thuds.

I squeeze my eyes shut and try to think of something else. Counting sheep never works, so instead I conjure the picture with my mom's name on the back, detail by detail. The puppy, the yard, the swing set, the peach tree, the wheelbarrow, the boat... Then, when I exhaust that image, I go over everything I can remember from my birth certificate. PLACE OF BIRTH: BARKBEE... MOTHER'S RESIDENCE: 6 CREEKSIDE ROAD, BARKBEE...

Then the floor tiles pop up again—those white octagons with orange and yellow petals, the black flourishes, mesmerizing me, hypnotizing me...

Except now the petals and flourishes start to move, swirling and snaking with streaks of red, until I think I see a face...

I jolt awake in the dark. The face evaporates—I can't conjure it now like I can the faces of Gladder Hill. But the feeling it gave me lingers. Like the feeling that tales of the mirror demon used to give me when I was little.

I wipe sweat from the back of my neck. I guess I'm still not free from children's stories.

"Ever wonder how many other people are out there?" Noah says. We're sitting cross-legged at the viewpoint—Noah playing with a yo-yo, and me practicing my Rubik's Cube. He nods at the land beyond.

I put down the Rubik's Cube and shield my eyes from the sun. "Sometimes," I say. *All the time.*

"My mom's from a place called New York City." Noah throws the yo-yo out and then back in again. "She said she hated it because there were too many people."

"Oh?" I turn to him. We rarely hear about places outside

Gladder Hill. And when we do, they're never described in a positive light. We know about Barkbee, obviously, and adults have said that there are other towns and cities outside Gladder Hill but none worth going to because no one has it as good as we do.

"Did she say how many people?" I ask.

Noah shakes his head. "I asked her, but she kind of brushed it off and changed the subject. Like she realized she'd said too much."

"How many do you think there are?"

"In New York City? Or total?"

"Total."

Noah does a yo-yo trick, swinging the string around his finger. "Maybe thousands?"

"*Thousands*?" I blink into the distance, trying to fathom so many people.

"Well, say there are at least ten other towns the size of Gladder Hill, or maybe bigger. That's at least a thousand. But who knows?" He rolls the yo-yo string up and tosses it in his bag.

"It's hard to imagine that many people," I say. "That many…" I hesitate.

"Faces?" Noah finishes for me. "Tell me about it."

My spine tingles. When was the last time someone mentioned faces out loud? Probably not since interiority lessons, and only because it was hard to teach us the importance of interiority—aka anti-Superficiality—without mentioning exteriors.

Questions that have always simmered inside me rise to my tongue now. I turn back to Noah. "Do you think they're *all* different, like they are here?"

Noah frowns. "Good question."

"It seems impossible."

"Why?"

"A hundred different faces is one thing. There can't be *thousands* of different faces, can there?" My head feels like it's going to explode with the thought.

"I don't know," he says. "But if every face is a different combo or permutation, that's a whole lot of permutations."

"Right. And—wait." I press my palm to my forehead. "Those thousands are only the thousands alive *today*. What about all the generations before that, since, like, the caveman days? That adds up to, like..."

"Infinity faces," Noah breathes.

And here I thought my collection of 102 faces would be such a big deal when done.

"Sometimes I think about other faces as much as my own," I admit.

"Well, at least we can *see* other faces." Noah twirls a desert dandelion between his fingers. "No way of seeing our own." He glances down at the shape in front of him on the grass. "Shadows seem to be the closest we can get."

"Yeah." I watch him twirl the dandelion back and forth, back and forth. "Although…"

"Although what?"

"Have you ever looked in someone else's eyes? The black part?"

The dandelion pauses in his fingers. "A couple of times," he says.

My heart thumps. "And what did you see?"

He looks up at me. "You've seen it too? A face?"

I nod.

"Are you saying…? Do you think it's…?"

"Well, I don't know for sure," I say. "But remember what Mr. Huttle said in physics once? About reflections? Certain surfaces—smooth and shiny ones…"

Noah leans forward, his Pop Eyes wide. "So we've both been thinking the same thing all this time?"

"I mean, there could just be tiny people living inside my grandma's eyes."

Noah laughs. "And my mom's too. Yeah, right."

"So you've gotten a good look before?"

"Well, I've tried when my mom kisses me good night. But she never stays close enough for long enough…"

"Yeah. It's either that or the lighting isn't right."

Noah clears this throat. "We could try it on each other."

"What?" My stomach lurches. "Right now?"

He shrugs, but he's twirling the dandelion faster and faster. "Why not?"

"Oh. Um. Sure, okay." I try to keep my voice steady.

"Okay." His eyes dart up toward me and then back down at the dandelion. My heart thumps harder. I wasn't expecting this. The possibility of Noah drawing me in a day or two was one thing, but if we're right about eye pupils, could I really get a look at myself right here, right now?

"Maybe we should count down," I mumble.

"Yeah. Good idea." Noah nods at the dandelion. "At the count of three, then?"

"Okay."

"Ready?"

I'm not sure *ready* is how I'd describe myself. This feels like it's happening too fast. And yet I've been waiting so long—wondering for years what I look like. How much readier can I be? And I might not get another chance to find out—at least until I'm eighteen, if I have the guts to leave Gladder Hill then. And that's ages away.

"I think so," I say. "You?"

"Think so."

"Okay."

Noah turns to face me. We both sit cross-legged, looking somewhere just past each other.

He clears his throat. "Here goes. One, two..."

My heart is pounding. Can he hear it?

"Three."

Noah shifts his gaze. I hold my breath as he leans toward me. I force myself to lean toward him too. The tips of our noses approach each other, and I try to focus on his eyes, his pupils. I can hear him swallow, can smell peanut butter on his breath. Our noses are almost touching now. I've never been this close to anyone besides Grandma, but this feels differ-ent... And why is *that* what I'm thinking about right now, when I'm supposed to be looking for the tiny face in his eyes?

My stomach starts to do backflips, then somersaults, and I don't know if that's because I'm about to see the tiny face or if there's another reason—does it have to do with Dr. Daya's talk?—but I try to concentrate. There it is, I see it—a shape bobbing, the tiniest of heads...well, two of them. I choose the one in Noah's right eye. But it's still so hard to see, so small, and I forgot pupils shrink in the sun, and the sun is bright, boring into me, making me squint, making Noah squint...

*Meow.*

We jerk apart and leap to our feet.

Tutu, the chiropractor's calico cat, meanders toward us.

Noah laughs, his voice cracking. "Scared the bejesus out of me."

"Me too." Tutu rubs against my leg, meowing, and I lean down to scratch behind her ears. And to avoid Noah's gaze. My heart still pounds. After it calms down a little, I straighten and glance at the sky. "I'd better get home." It's mostly a true statement—Grandma likes me home before suppertime.

"Same. See you tomorrow for the drawing lesson?"

"Sounds good."

We mumble goodbye without looking at each other. As I head home, my heart rate takes forever to slow down. And I'm still not sure if it's because I came so close to glimpsing something in Noah's pupils—or so close to Noah.

# 12

WHERE DO I BEGIN?

Noah sits cross-legged next to me on my bed, waiting for me to explain how to draw a face. I was worried things would be awkward after the eye incident, but we've been pretending it never happened, and aside from not meeting each other's eyes, we seem to have fallen back into our normal banter. For now.

I stare at the blank page in my sketchbook and think over everything I've learned since starting my collection. Everything I've taught myself.

"Well," I say finally. "I don't know if this is the best technique, but I usually start by closing my eyes and picturing whoever I'm drawing. And then—"

"Whoa," Noah interrupts. "That's how you draw everyone? Completely from memory?"

"Well, yeah. I can't exactly sit in front of them while I draw."

"I guess not. But how can your memory be that good?"

"It's only that good if I've seen the person recently. Name someone we saw today, and I'll draw them."

Noah sits back and strokes his chin. "How about Principal Gladder?"

"Already did her." I flip to her sketch in my collection.

He studies the sketch. "Uncanny. How about Mr. Huttle, then?"

"Okay. I haven't done him yet." I conjure an image of Mr. Huttle in my mind from class today and then start to draw, beginning with his eyes and the purple pouches under them. Then I form his nose and mouth, with the extra-large space between them. Suddenly I feel conscious of Noah watching my pencil's every move. No one has ever watched me draw a face before. I mess up a bunch of lines and have to do a lot of erasing and redrawing.

When I finally finish, I turn it toward him.

"Wow." Noah stares at my drawing. "That's him all right. It's official: you're a magician."

I shrug, but inside I'm beaming.

"I don't think I can do that," he says.

"Sure you can. Here, try drawing the last person you saw up close. Besides me." I flip to a blank page and watch him close his eyes for a second. Then he opens them and starts to draw. I wince as he draws the head first—a *circle*—and then puts the eyes—almond shapes—too far apart and the mouth too low to be any human I've seen. He doesn't use any shading; the sketch is completely one-dimensional.

"Done. Can you tell who it is?"

I try to guess. "Mr. Lorry?"

He frowns. "No."

"Your dad?"

He scrunches up his nose. "It's Mrs. Scorsetti."

I may have my work cut out for me.

Noah hangs his head.

"It's okay. It takes practice." I try to be encouraging, as if we're doing partner critiques in art class. "And when we draw each other, we can do it live instead of from memory, so it won't be as hard." I flip to my sketch of Mr. Mackafee. "Try copying this. But don't start with a circle."

"What should I start with?"

"I usually start with the nose or the eyes and then build out from there. Sometimes I make little dots and grid lines to mark where the other parts should be. You can erase the lines later." I take the pencil and show him what I mean on a blank page. "Proportion is everything. My sketches never look right if I don't get the proportions right. You have to think about anatomy."

"Anatomy?"

"Like, when you look at a face from the front, the ears are about the same level as the nose, right? And the space between the eyes is usually as wide as one eye. But that all changes a little depending on the person..."

Noah's Pop Eyes bulge again. "You've given faces a *lot* of thought, huh?"

There's something about the way he says that. My cheeks grow hot. "What, am I too Superficial even for you?"

"That's not what I'm saying."

"Well, if you don't want to learn—"

"I'm just impressed is all. Honestly. Keep going." He presses his palms together and lifts his hands. "Please?"

I puff out my cheeks. I'm not sure why I got so defensive, but I try to shake it off. "All right, fine. Why don't you trace this first? Then you can give it a shot on your own."

I get out some tracing paper, and he traces my version of Mr. Mackafee. Then I have him try copying it on a blank sheet. The copy he makes looks a bit lopsided, but it's better than his attempt at Mrs. Scorsetti. I have him copy a few more faces in my collection, giving him tips here and there, until the third one finally looks similar to its original. Or at least close enough.

"See, you're getting the hang of it," I say.

Noah grins. "I guess this is what happens when you have an art teacher who actually knows what they're talking about. So does this mean I'm ready?" He flips to a blank page and holds the pencil over it, looking at me.

My heart starts to thump. "Ready for what?"

He laughs. "What do you think?"

I glance at the clock. "We don't have time. My grandma will be home any minute."

"I thought we had till four thirty. That's ten minutes."

"You'll be rushed. And sometimes she gets in early."

Noah's shoulders droop. "How about tomorrow?"

"She doesn't work again till Tuesday."

"Tuesday, then?"

"Okay." I close my collection, trying not to sound relieved. Something slips out of the sketchbook and falls onto the bed.

"What's that?" He snatches it up before I can.

"Nothing." I try to take it back from him. "I found it in my grandma's room."

He holds the picture of the puppy away from me.

"Doesn't look like nothing. Is it a painting? Or a drawing? Or what?"

I chew on my lip. Now that he's brought up the topic, I realize how much I've been wanting to talk to someone about it. "I was wondering the same thing," I say. "It doesn't seem like either one."

Noah flips the picture over and frowns. "Sierra Photography Studio? What's that?"

"I don't know exactly, but..." I hesitate. "Sierra's my mom's name. I also found her address on my birth certificate. It's in Barkbee."

"Wow. Have you ever met her?"

I shake my head. "My grandma said she abandoned me."

Noah's grip on the picture tightens. I take it from him before he crinkles it. "Why would she do that?" he says.

"I'd like to know myself." I put the picture back in my sketchbook, taping it to the inside back cover so it won't fall out again.

"Well, when we're eighteen, we should go find her." Noah punches the air. "Demand an explanation."

"We?" I kneel next to my bed and slip the sketchbook back in the shoebox and under the floorboard.

"Only if you want moral support."

I grin. An explanation would be nice—though the thought of meeting my mom gives me more butterflies. I've noticed that some kids in Gladder Hill resemble their parents or sibling. I don't have a sibling, but if I were to see my mom, it might give me some idea… Not that it matters, if Noah is going to draw me tomorrow anyway, but still, the thought of meeting her—

I hear a key card beeping, the front door opening. Noah and I exchange a look. I glance around my room, even though I just put my collection away. There's no trace of what we've been doing.

"Hey, kiddo," Grandma calls. "You home?"

"Come on." I head to my door and beckon Noah to follow. He grabs his backpack, and we hurry into the kitchen just as Grandma sets her key card on the table.

She blinks at Noah, her smile fading. "Oh. You have company."

"Hi, ma'am." Noah fidgets. "Zailey was just helping me with homework."

"Yep," I say. "Math."

Why is Grandma watching Noah with her eyes all narrow like that? Maybe she's having trouble seeing again. She really should try wearing contact lenses.

Grandma crosses her arms. "You're supposed to be

doing your own homework at the kitchen table, Azalea. Like we agreed."

"But you weren't home yet."

"I don't care."

Noah coughs. "I was just heading out. Nice to see you, ma'am." He nods at Grandma and then waves at me. "Later."

"Bye," I mumble.

Grandma watches him slip by her and out the door. Then she turns to me. "I don't like that."

"Like what?" I frown. "Why were you so rude to him?"

"You shouldn't be home alone with another kid without adult supervision."

"Why not? It's just Noah." I try to keep my voice light and innocent, as if Noah and I weren't secretly drawing people and discussing each other's Superficial thoughts. "You weren't like this when Olive used to come over."

"That was different." Grandma hesitates. "Noah's a boy, and you're getting older now…"

My stomach flips. Does this have to do with Dr. Daya's talk? She'd mentioned that boys and girls might start thinking about each other differently, but she didn't explain that part well, and then she read through some pamphlet about "relationships" and how people who love each other and get married and maybe have kids should do so because they're attracted to each other's personalities, and she mentioned how, when we're eighteen, we can start dating other kids in Gladder Hill if we want to, after we take compatibility tests. I didn't understand what this had to do with changing bodies, and to be honest, I still don't.

Grandma clears her throat. "Just don't do that again. Okay?"

"But—"

"That's the end of the conversation. Now I want you to finish your homework out here. And I want to see it when it's done."

I sigh and spread my homework out on the kitchen table. But my mind drifts, thinking about ways Noah and I can still carry out our plan on Tuesday. The neighbors might see Noah coming over and mention it to Grandma. He'll have to sneak through the bushes and into the backyard and come in that way. Yeah, that could work. And we'll have to make sure we don't take as long as we did today. Grandma will still get home from work around four thirty. We had enough time for our lesson this afternoon; we'll have enough time on Tuesday too.

Only on Tuesday, it won't be a lesson. On Tuesday, I'll get an answer. I'll meet the face I've been walking around with my whole life. The face that my schoolmates, my teachers, everyone in Gladder Hill has seen every day. On Tuesday, I'll find out what lies beyond the Uncrossable Boundary after years of wondering. Years of envisioning all kinds of possibilities. A round face. A square face. A beak nose like Grandma's or a tomato face like Mr. Wallus's. A speckled face like Hal Gotwell's or a plain one like Principal Gladder's. Which one am I hoping for?

The truth is, I don't know. I just know I want to know what other people see when they talk to me—or even think of me. Because when *I* think of someone—when a particular person crosses my mind for whatever reason—I picture their face first. It's not like I do it on purpose. My mind just does it.

But on Tuesday, I won't have to wonder anymore. Finally, at last, I'll know my whole self. And that's the point, isn't it? Simply to know.

# 13

I F IT WAS HARD to concentrate in school before, it's impossible now.

"Please rise for the Gladder Hill pledge." Principal Gladder's voice on the loudspeaker sounds calm as ever—the opposite of my mind and all the thoughts bouncing around it. It doesn't help that I brought my collection to school again. But Grandma isn't working today, and I noticed she tidied my room the other day when I wasn't there. So lately I'd rather lock the sketchbook in my locker—and just be extra careful transferring it—than leave it unguarded at home.

*On my honor, I will strive*

*To be kind to myself and others—*

I glance sidelong at Noah.

*To focus on substance, not surface—*

His eyes flit toward me.

*With regard to all people—*

We hold each other's gaze for a second. A gaze of

shared secrets. Shared guilt. But the shared part almost makes it...fun?

*And to uphold the values of Gladder Hill.*

We pull our eyes back to the front of the room.

"Now for today's announcements. The Rubik's Cube race will be held at two o'clock in room fourteen..."

Shoot, I forgot about the race. They only happen once a month, and this month I've been a little distracted. I'll have to practice during lunchtime.

But lunchtime takes forever to arrive as the minutes inch by. Noah and I pass notes during class when the teacher isn't looking—nothing that would give us away, of course, if they were to be intercepted.

Is your grandma still mad?

*A little, but she'll get over it.*

Should I still come over tomorrow? I'd offer my house, but my dad's always around...

*Sure, as long as we finish before she gets home from work.*

Ok. Wanna hang out at the viewpoint after school today?

*I've got the Rubik's Cube race, then homework.* ☹

Ooh, right. Good luck with the race!

*Thanks. You should join the RC club and race with us.*

Nah, I prefer chess club. Not that a cube made of smaller cubes isn't exciting...

And a square board covered with smaller squares is?

Touché.

By the time two o'clock rolls around, the last thing I want to do is the Rubik's Cube race, but I try to get my mind in the zone. I pull out my cube for some last-minute practice in the hall. In my head I go over the strategies we learned in club meetings: *Make the white cross, then do the first and middle layers, then get the top corners...* And I give myself a pep talk: *You can do it. You are capable of thinking about non-Superficial things for one minute and ten seconds.*

One minute and ten seconds is my personal record; I got third place in the last race, after Jen Rosenthal and Malorie Windleson, who holds the school record at thirty-two seconds. I don't think I'll ever beat her, but it was cool to place. And it made me feel like I was good at something besides art.

We take our seats at the round table in room fourteen, all ten of us. Jill isn't in the club, but Olive is, and she sits next to me now. We smile at each other. I don't know how

I feel about her anymore or how she feels about me; in Wonderland it seemed clear that she wouldn't approve of the real me, the one who thinks about life outside Gladder Hill. But we make small talk now anyway, joking about how we forgot to practice, releasing our nervous pre-race energy on each other.

Mr. Huttle, who runs the club, calls for our attention and reminds us of the rules—don't distract others, don't touch the cubes till he says go, etcetera. Then he places the prize at the center of the table: the fancy neon glow-in-the-dark Rubik's Cube I saw in the general store. We ogle it as he pulls shuffled Rubik's Cubes out of a bag and sets one before each of us.

He raises his stopwatch. "Okay, guys. Get ready... Get set..."

Everyone looks down at their cubes, already assessing the top side. I probably should too—

"Go!"

We seize our cubes. Malorie's hands start working at lightning speed to my left. I notice how my arm looks next to hers—how much more hair mine has. No, stop that, back to the cube... Two red squares there, two blues there...but how do I get that green square to go there? I glance up; across from me, Josh Fonteau's lips press together in concentration, hiding the gap in his teeth. Which reminds me, I haven't added him to my collection yet...

No, back to the cube!

I'm doomed. Solving a Rubik's Cube takes intense focus, but my attention span seems shorter than ever lately. Except when I'm working on my face collection.

"Finished." Malorie drops her cube and raises her hands.

Josh curses under his breath.

"Way to go, Malorie," Mr. Huttle says, pressing buttons on his stopwatch. "Everyone else keep going."

"Done," Josh declares after a few seconds.

My palms start to sweat. Sweaty hands aren't good for handling Rubik's Cubes. *Focus, focus.*

"Me too," says Ricky.

I won't place this time. What if I don't even come in fourth? What if I come in last—what if everyone is waiting awkwardly and I can't solve my cube at all? What if it's true that I can only focus on surface, not substance, and don't belong in "such an intellectual community," as Grandma called it?

Fear drives my fingers and brain now. Finally, more and more of the same colors clump together on my cube. Green joins green, blue joins blue...and then *bam,* at last, each side is one color. "Finished," I squeak, relief flooding me. Fourth place. Worse than last time, but only by a margin. I'm not completely hopeless, not entirely unworthy of Gladder Hill's intellectual prestige.

Mick Scalini finishes after me, followed by everyone else, one by one, until Hal takes last place. Then we all break into excited post-race chatter. "Good race, everyone," Mr. Huttle says as he hands Malorie her prize. She offers to let everyone borrow it, insisting in her modest way that we're all winners.

As I head home, I promise myself I'll practice my Rubik's Cube more often. I'll practice the cello more too, and study harder, spend more time on homework—do as much as I can to balance out my Superficial activities, like my face collection and the lessons with Noah. I'll make sure drawing faces isn't my only skill. After all, is being good at something bad even a skill?

A golf cart zooms past me on Main Street, throwing up a dust cloud from the dirt road. I cough. "Sorry, Zailey," I hear Mr. Aberdeen call.

As the cloud clears, I glimpse him in the driver's seat and old Mr. Cruz looking back from the passenger seat.

"Sorry, dear," he shouts. "My fault, I told him to pick up the speed. Late for bingo."

I can't help laughing, even with a new layer of dirt coating me. Now I'm not just sweaty but dirty too.

Grandma is snoring on the couch when I get home. She's left a greasy pot on the stove and a dirty dish in the sink from whatever she made for lunch. I don't mind; she deserves to be lazy on her days off.

I throw down my backpack in my room, peel off my clothes, and hurry into the bathroom. I can't wait to get in the shower and wash away the dirt and sweat. I don't usually take long showers, but today I let the hot water work up steam, until the skin on my fingertips shrivels and I can feel all the drain holes pressing tiny circles into the soles of my feet. I massage my scalp with shampoo, rinse it, and then wash my face—

My fingers pause on my chin. The bump is gone.

It was there when I woke up this morning. And I swear it was there when I checked before the race. But I don't feel a trace of it now.

Maybe I imagined it. Or has it turned into something that can be seen but not felt?

If it's really gone, I'll never know what it looked like; that question will never be answered. On the other hand, my face feels like its familiar self again. I turn off the shower and remind myself that it doesn't matter. I dry myself with a towel and wrap it around me, tucking it in near my armpits, and head back toward my room.

I pause in the hall. My bedroom door is open. Did I leave it that way?

I hear a shuffling sound and rush to the doorway. Grandma is standing in my room with her back to me. A laundry basket sits at her feet with my dusty clothes and dirty backpack in it.

My backpack. Its contents have been emptied onto the bed, except for...

I hear a page turn, and another. I step into the room and see it in Grandma's hands: the pocket-size sketchbook. My face collection.

No, no, no.

She turns to me, her lips tight, her knuckles white. She holds out the open sketchbook: Miss Ellowby's and Ricky Sanchez's faces. She's near the beginning but at least a dozen faces in.

"Care to explain?" she says through her teeth.

I clutch a fistful of my towel. "Why were you snooping in my room?"

I know I'm deflecting, but it's all I can think to say.

A sound erupts from somewhere in Grandma's throat, a laugh gone wrong. "Well. I was 'snooping,' as you call it, because I saw that your bag and clothes were filthy. Thought I'd wash them for you." She snaps the sketchbook shut. "But I found something filthier."

A chill runs up my spine, and I don't think it's the air-conditioning.

"Is *this* what you were doing with Noah? Is he the one who got you into this?"

I hesitate. That's probably what she prefers to think: someone else must have lured me to the dark side. No granddaughter of hers would have gotten this idea on her own. I bet she wants to believe it so badly that if I said yes now—if I blamed this on Noah—she'd eat up the lie in a heartbeat. And maybe I'd be less of a disgrace in her eyes.

But what would that mean for Noah? Would Grandma tell his parents or Principal Gladder? Noah would hate me forever, and maybe his family would get evicted like Mr. Grinwold did. I may be a bad seed already, but that would be going too far.

"No," I say. "I started it all on my own."

Grandma's jaw shifts. "I thought I raised you right. I thought here you could never..." Tears well up in her eyes.

"Why would you do this?"

I twist a corner of my towel. "They're just sketches. I only wanted to—"

"Do you want to turn out like your mother?"

I stare at her. "How am I supposed to know when you won't tell me anything about her?"

"Well, you can forget this little hobby." She waves the sketchbook in the air. "You'll never so much as doodle again, do you understand me?" She pushes past me into the hall.

"What?" I sputter. "That's not fair." I follow her as she bounds across the kitchen to the stove, turning on a front gas burner. Before I realize what she's doing, she dips a corner of my sketchbook through the flame, turns off the burner, and chucks the sketchbook in the greasy pot next to it. She grabs a bottle of cooking oil and pours some into the pot. I watch her clamp the lid on the pot and walk away, brushing her hands together.

My breath catches. The picture is taped inside—the picture with my mom's name on the back. The only piece of her I have. And maybe the only piece of her Grandma has.

All my sketches can be redrawn, all my hard work redone, but that image...

*No.* I lunge past Grandma and grab the handle of the pot

lid and lift it, hoping I can salvage the picture if I dump the sketchbook in the sink.

"Zailey, don't—" Grandma's shout cuts out as a burst of orange rushes up from the pot, engulfing me.

Engulfing everything.

Flaming teeth—

I stumble.

—tearing into me—

*Make it stop.*

—gnawing, chewing—

It won't stop.

—screaming—

Yes, someone keeps screaming, and I wish they'd shut up so I can think. It's so hard to think...

As the world turns inward and darkens, a thought flickers once: maybe the someone is me.

# PART II

SPEC·U·LAR

*adjective*

1. of, relating to, or having the properties of a mirror

# 14

B*EEEEP.*

    *Beeeep.*

*Beeeep.*

The sound drips into my consciousness like drops of water falling from a faucet. Dull thuds at first, solidifying into soft, high-pitched notes, tapping my eardrums every few seconds. What is making that noise?

But opening my eyes seems like too much work just yet. I can feel some sort of blanket or sheet on my arms and legs, scratchy, unfamiliar. Whatever I'm wearing, too, rubs a bit rough against my skin. These aren't my clothes. This isn't my bed.

This isn't Gladder Hill.

Voices float over the beeping.

"Mostly second-degree. Some third." A voice I don't know. A man's. "So there may be some nerve damage. But her airways all appear intact, luckily. We did the initial cleansing and medicating while she was under the anesthesia."

"Initial? What else is there to do?" A voice I do know. Grandma's. Muffled, a bit off, but definitely hers.

"Well, we'll do another assessment today when she wakes up. Check her vision too. And skin grafting surgery would be the next consideration, after the bandages come off."

"Skin grafting?"

"It would minimize scarring and even help with—"

"That doesn't sound necessary to me. She should go back to Gladder Hill as soon as possible."

The man clears his throat. "Look, I understand you're not supposed to be concerned about how she'll look. I know it's against your religion—"

"Religion? Gladder Hill isn't a religion."

"Okay, well, I'm just saying, no one *here* will judge you if you go ahead with the surgery. And I recommend that you do, because—"

"Of course you do. It will make you more money, won't it?" Grandma's voice strains in a way I've never heard it do before. "I shouldn't have brought her here. I took the risk so she could get the best care, but all you people care about out here is money and looks. Plastic surgery—"

"I promise you that's quite a different thing. There are practical reasons to—"

"You said this was the most Gladder Hill–friendly room in the hospital. Shouldn't that include the doctor working in it?"

"Ma'am, I completely respect your lifestyle. I just want you to understand—"

"I'm sorry, I need to step out."

The man sighs. "Right, of course. I know this is a lot to process. I'll give you some time while I check on another patient."

"Where is the cafeteria?"

"Ground floor."

"Will someone be here while I'm gone? In case she wakes up?"

"Of course," says a new voice—a woman's. "I'll be looking after her."

"Yes, Lydia will be here."

"Okay."

Feet shuffle. A door clicks open and closed.

*Beeeep. Beeeep. Beeeep.*

With fewer sounds distracting me now, my attention returns to what I feel. The mattress I'm lying on is a bit firmer than I'm used to, and my upper body rests at an incline. There's something wrapped around my upper left arm. And my head—my face—feels scratchy and stifled. As if something encases it.

I force my eyes open, blinking. My surroundings come into focus: a white wall opposite me. Bright fluorescent lights above. The shapes of my legs protruding under a white blanket. A gray piece of plastic clipped onto my left middle finger, connected by a wire to some sort of small machine next to me, with a green light that blinks in sync with the beeping. But it all looks half there. I glimpse the edges of white material in my periphery.

Panic flutters in my chest. I reach up, groping for the textures my fingertips know, the familiar feel of my chin and cheeks and nose. Instead they encounter a scratchy surface. It's all around—it's covering my left eye too. The panic quickens from a flutter to a thrash.

"No, no, sweetie, don't touch your bandages." A woman dressed in medical scrubs appears beside the bed, smiling. A round and rosy face, one I don't know—and yet a bit like Miss Pewter's from school. For some reason, that comforts me as I lie in this strange room. "Glad to see you're awake," the woman says.

"Why is my left eye covered?" I croak. You'd think I hadn't spoken in a year. And as I move my mouth, I realize how tight and sore my face feels under the bandages.

"It's just for a little while. Don't worry, the doctor will

explain everything when he gets back." The woman pats my arm. She has long hair the color of straw, and it's pulled back low behind her neck rather than hanging around her face like the tour girl Beryl's hair. I want to reach out and touch it, but I stop myself. "I'm Lydia, by the way," she says. "Your nurse. How are you feeling?"

"Thirsty."

"No doubt." Lydia picks up a weird cup that I didn't notice sitting on the bedside tray. "We gave you fluids through an IV while you were out before. But it's important to stay hydrated. Here, have some water."

The papery cup she lifts is open at the top—not like Gladder Hill's spill-proof sip cups. Is it safe to drink uncovered like that? We've always been told that the longer water, or any liquid, is exposed to open air once poured from its source, the less safe it is to drink or use.

But she's a nurse; she wouldn't give a patient unsanitary water, would she?

My thirst overpowers my hesitance as she guides a straw between my lips. I take long sips, draining the whole thing in seconds, even though it stings a bit going down my throat.

"Feel a little better now?"

I nod. "Where am I?"

She puts the cup back on the tray. "Sunrise Children's Hospital."

There's definitely no place by that name in Gladder Hill. We only have one medical center, and it's for everyone, both children and adults.

"I don't remember getting here," I say.

She unwraps the thing around my upper arm—a blood pressure cuff, I realize, also connected to that beeping machine. "I'm sure the helicopter ride was a blur."

"Helicopter?" I stare at her. I've never been in a helicopter, let alone an airplane. I've only seen them as specks in the distance—only imagined what it was like to be in one and watch the world from that height.

She writes something down on a clipboard. "Mm-hmm, you were airlifted."

My jaw drops. I can't believe I traveled by helicopter and wasn't conscious to remember it—just my luck. "Why?" I ask.

Lydia removes my finger clip. "Well, they don't have the equipment or expertise in Gladder Hill to treat your kind of burns. Your grandma had to make a quick decision."

I swallow; my throat stings again. "Burns?"

She looks at me, her eyes softening. "You had an accident yesterday. Do you remember?"

*A flash of orange, a rush of heat...*

My stomach twists. All at once, I remember it too well—the moment before the world went black. I've had burns before, on my tongue and my hands, from eating food before it cooled or turning the sink faucet too hot, and there was always that flinch, that intake of breath, that one shot of pain. But this time it wasn't one shot. It just kept going. And going. My fingers wander up to my bandages again.

"Uh-uh." Lydia wags a finger at me. "Remember what I said, sweetie? Hands off your dressings. It will only be for a couple of weeks."

"A couple of weeks? Why do I need them on?"

"To avoid infection and irritation." She leans past me to adjust my pillows. "They'll need changing in a week. The doctor will explain everything, okay?" I notice the badge on her chest. A picture, a face. I squint. It looks almost exactly like the face sitting in front of me: so crisp, clear, and lifelike...like the picture that I found in Grandma's room. The picture that, I remember with a twinge, was tucked inside my burning sketchbook.

I push that thought out of my mind and focus on the

badge. It has a name on it: *Lydia Whelan, RN*. And below it: *Sunrise Children's Hospital of Barkbee*.

Wait a minute. Barkbee?

My heart races as Lydia pats my arm and smiles. "You just relax and rest. Your grandma went to get a refreshment, I think, and should be back soon. I need to run some numbers over to the front desk. I'll only be a few minutes, but just press that button there if you need anything, okay?"

Lydia leaves the room through the only door in here. The room itself is white and windowless and no bigger than my bedroom at home. Lydia told me to rest, but my body fidgets. My mind races.

I'm beyond the gates.

I'm in Barkbee. I'm near my mom. Or at least near the address she listed on my birth certificate. 6 CREEKSIDE ROAD, BARKBEE...

Never in a million years would I have guessed this is how I'd get out of Gladder Hill. I thought there was no way out until I was eighteen. After years of glimpsing the gates open and close once a week for imports, all of it carefully monitored, I'd resigned myself.

But it turns out there is a way, and Grandma, of all people, gave me the key. She must be kicking herself now.

Grandma—she'll be back any minute. And the thought of seeing her, talking to her… My whole body clenches, remembering what happened, the way she talked to me and forbade me from drawing and threw my sketchbook in the fire, the fire that caused that agony, the fire that *she* caused…

I toss back the bedcover. I'm wearing a hospital gown. I look around the room and notice Grandma's green duffel bag in the corner; there might be some normal clothes in there. I climb out of the bed. It feels good to stretch my legs. A band around my wrist displays my name and date of birth; I yank at it, harder and harder until it snaps off. Then I walk over to the duffel bag and unzip it, finding Grandma's heart medication, some pajamas, and—hallelujah—a pair of my pants, my sneakers, and one of my T-shirts. It's all in a jumble. I imagine Grandma throwing stuff into the bag as she waited for the helicopter to arrive. How much time did she have? Was I passed out already or still screaming? Did anyone else see me before I was put in the helicopter? I shudder.

I pull out the pants and T-shirt and change into them, careful not to rub the shirt against my bandages as I pull it over my head. *Infection…irritation…* The nurse's words didn't sound pleasant.

I'm not wearing socks, and it looks like Grandma forgot

to pack any—but better to have no socks than no shoes. I put on the sneakers and straighten, breathing out. The change of clothes makes a huge difference. I feel more like myself now. Except for the bandages on my face, that is.

I go to the door and turn the knob. It feels cold and smooth, sort of like our blue lockers at school, only it's grayish and shinier—shinier than any surface I've seen before. But I don't have time to dwell on it. I inch the door open and peek through the crack. A few people walk by wearing medical scrubs and staring at clipboards. Once they pass, I open the door wider. My heart beats faster. So far all I've experienced of the world outside the gates is one room. Four white walls. And that's probably all Grandma intends for me to experience before she takes me back to Gladder Hill. I heard what she said to the doctor: *She should go back to Gladder Hill as soon as possible.*

She certainly doesn't intend for me to find my mom.

I think of Noah's words, his hand punching the air. *We should go find her. Demand an explanation.* My stomach sinks a little knowing he's not here.

But I'm here, and this is an opportunity I don't get every day.

I slip out of the room while the coast is clear. The hall

stretches long and bright before me. So far, Sunrise Children's Hospital could be a building in Gladder Hill. It has walls, a floor, a ceiling, and doors. It's not as if I'm on another planet. There's nothing that strange except more of those extra-shiny doorknobs.

I turn a corner and almost bump into a nurse with a clipboard. She looks up and blinks. "Pardon me. Do you need help with something?"

"Um, no," I mumble. "I'm just—"

"Aren't you one of Dr. Kahue's patients? Are you supposed to be out of your room?"

Too many questions. "Yep, all good," I mumble, hurrying past her. Voices rise behind me. I dart around a corner and spot a Toilet sign ahead above an open door. It has weird symbols on it, but the word *toilet* is all I need to see. I throw myself inside and lock the door, leaning on it with my palms. *Deep breaths. Inhale, exhale.* I feel for the light switch and flip it. As I turn, something moves above the sink. I squeal and jump back.

"Sorry, I didn't know someone else was..." I trail off. A face stares back at me—though I can't tell if it's like any I've seen before.

Because it's covered in bandages.

# 15

THE STRANGER BLINKS AT me. Or at least one eye does. The other hides behind the bandages: white strips wrapped over not just the left eye, but also the forehead, temples, cheeks, jaws, chin, and nose, with an opening for the nostrils… The only other part of the face they don't cover, aside from one eye, is the lips—thin, chapped ones.

"What the…?" I start to say. The stranger's lips move at the same time mine do. But I don't hear another voice, only my own.

The person appears to be staring at me through a rectangular opening in the wall above the sink, looking out from another bathroom. The rectangle cuts off anything below the elbows, but I can see that the person is wearing a T-shirt like mine—same color, same font. Only it says something different:

ꓱverꓗone's glaꓷꓷeꤕ in ꓧlaꓷꓷeꤕ ꓧill

What language is that? Wait—I read it again. One of the

characters resembles a backward *n*. Another, a flipped *r*…a reversed *e*…

My body tingles.

Could this rectangle be what I think it is?

I take a step forward. The stranger steps toward me at the same time. I try to trick her—try to turn my head especially fast—but I can't get ahead of her. She misses nothing. Every movement I make she makes too, in reverse, at the same time. Not a moment sooner or later.

I hold my breath and reach out, my hand coming toward the stranger's until…until… I gasp. There it is. My fingertips meet a cool, hard surface. Not an opening in the wall at all.

The stranger and I lower our hands.

I think of the few mirror rumors I've heard over the years. One claimed that mirrors imitate your motions, like shadows do. Another rumor—that they'll show you a clear image of yourself—sounded too much like magic. The sort of thing I'd have to see for myself to believe.

I never heard anything about the image reversing horizontally, but this person before me has a hangnail on her right pointer finger, like the one on my left. And—I pull up my sleeve—a brown mark below her left shoulder, like the one below my right. And—I pull up my shirt—a mark from chickenpox on the right side of her stomach like the one on my left. And the same dark hair on both of her arms.

I lean forward over the sink, and the mirror girl—if that's what she is—leans toward me. The one eye I can see is brown, not hazel like Grandma's, and a teeny streak of red runs through the white part of the eye. The eyelashes are black, like the hair on my arms and legs. My hand trembles a little as it reaches up to my cheek, to the bandages. The mirror girl's hand does the same.

*Thwack, thwack, thwack.*

I jump and drop my hand. So does the mirror girl.

"Zailey? Are you in there?"

Panic sets my heart racing. How long have I been staring at her?

"This is Dr. Kahue." I recognize the voice behind the door—it belongs to the man who was talking to Grandma earlier. "If you're in there, we need you to come back to your room, please," Dr. Kahue says. "For your own health and safety."

Safety? I was supposed to be safe in Gladder Hill, and look where that landed me—in a hospital with bandages on my face. And Grandma will *never* take her eyes off me if I go back to her now. She'll watch me like a hawk until we're back in Gladder Hill—and once we're there, she'll keep watching my every move until I'm eighteen at least, making sure I don't draw. Or meet my mom.

*Thwack, thwack, thwack.* The doorknob jiggles.

I tear my uncovered eye from the mirror girl and look around. There's an opening in the wall, some sort of window, there, above the radiator. I can see through it to the trees outside—no shutters. Weird. I reach up and—*ouch*. My hand bumps into something hard. There *is* something there—a transparent panel. I can make out smudges of dust or grime on it. As I rise onto my tiptoes and peer closer, I glimpse a figure too, flickering against the backdrop of trees. A head with bandages. The mirror girl again?

"Zailey?" Grandma's voice booms now. "Azalea, are you in there? Come out now, please."

I'll come out, all right—just not the way she wants me to. I notice the lever on the window and pull it, trying to ignore the flickers of the mirror girl. Pulling it doesn't work. I push it. The clear panel moves. I feel a breeze. So this is how you open a window in the outside world.

I hoist myself up onto the radiator and then the sill. The knocking grows louder.

"We'll have to force the door open if no one comes out," I hear the doctor say. "We'd rather not."

I glance back at the mirror girl above the sink—one last look. Her lips press together, something I do when I'm nervous. Then I turn and swing my legs through the window, wriggling my body out. It's lucky I'm on the ground floor. I land on my feet on pavement. I squint in the sun. I must be at the rear of the hospital, because there's nothing around except some dumpsters and then woods.

There's only one way to go from here—unless I want to go back to Gladder Hill, back to so-called "safety."

So into the woods I go, even as my heart hammers in my chest.

# 16

GLADDER HILL CONTAINS FOUR streets, thirty-nine houses, and one apartment building. I can name each street and tell you who lives in every house and apartment. It's not hard to keep track.

But as I stand now at the edge of the woods some fifteen minutes from Sunrise Children's Hospital, question marks line the street in front of me: strange houses belonging to strangers.

And I don't know whether they scare or excite me.

I step out of the trees and start walking down the cul-de-sac, gazing at the houses on either side of me. In some ways, they aren't that unlike Gladder Hill houses. They have doors and roofs and chimneys. Again, it's not as if I'm on another planet.

But these houses are bigger, and in the places where our shuttered wall openings would sit, square and rectangle panels glint in the sun. They must be like the window in the hospital bathroom.

But that's just the outside; it's hard to guess what the houses might be like inside. Houses are like faces in a way. They have this public exterior that's always the first thing you see—the first thing you really know about whoever lives there. But inside is the private part, the part that tells you what the inhabitants are really like. The part that only certain people—people invited in—get to see. I think of Grandma's purple paradise bedroom that no one would ever guess was in our bungalow just by looking at the plain brown outside with its chipping paint, which isn't too inviting if I think about it. Kind of like Grandma herself: narrowed eyes and a straight mouth seem to be her default setting, but she can make you laugh so hard during a game of charades. And cook you omelets with your favorite fillings. And hug you when you're feeling sad or even just because.

*Don't think about Grandma. Don't think about home.*

I force my attention back to the houses here. Aside from their weird windows and bigger size, they also have more grass around them. Green grass—at least greener than the little that grows in Gladder Hill. In one yard to my left, a rotating machine sprinkles water on the lawn. These houses also have longer, wider driveways. A red vehicle sits in one to my right. I recognize it as a type of motor vehicle I've sometimes spotted from the viewpoint in Gladder Hill, coming down the long road to the delivery gates, though never past them. A *car*. A *van*. A *truck*. I've heard the adults use these words, and although I looked them up in the dictionary once, I can't always remember the difference between them. I think this red one's a car. I usually hear the vehicles coming because they're louder than the golf carts and power chairs and bikes people use to get around Gladder Hill. But I've never seen one up close.

I take a few more steps toward the red car now, staring at its glossy surface. I walk around to the side of the vehicle. Something moves on a little wing sticking out. I freeze, glimpsing my T-shirt but with the backward words again.

**ꞮꞮiH ɿǝbbɒlⅅ ni ɿǝbbɒlǫ ꙅ'ǝnoγɿǝvꓱ**

And other non-backward words: *Objects in mirror are closer than they appear.*

Well, if I had any doubt about what a mirror is, here's my confirmation.

I step toward it and reach out. My fingertips merge with the mirror girl's and meet a smooth, hard surface like the one in the hospital bathroom. I didn't expect mirrors to feel this way. I don't know what I expected. Maybe I thought my hand would go through it—like the mirror demon reaching through in those tales. Those lies, more like it. No demon has

grabbed me and pulled me through to some dark, cold otherworld. What other lies have adults told us?

A whirring sound rises behind me. I turn. It's another
car, blue, moving down the street. It slows as it approaches
me, and I see two people peering at me from inside: a woman
at the wheel and a man in the seat next to her.

It occurs to me I probably shouldn't be standing here.
I hurry away down the sidewalk, fixing my right eye on the
end of the street. The hum of the motor behind me stops. I
dare to glance over my shoulder. The blue car is now parked
at the house opposite the red car. I relax. It isn't following me.

The man and the woman get out, carrying bags and
wearing strange clothes: the woman, a tight-fitting garment
that stops at her knees—no pants!—and the man, a looser
shirt tucked into dark-blue pants. The woman glances my
way again, and I jerk my head back. I really hope this isn't
Creekside Road. I don't know why, but I'd rather my mom
live on any street but this one.

When I come to the end, the sign there says PEONY
CIRCLE. *Phew*.

The road turns left onto another dead end, so I turn
right. ROSEBUD WAY. I follow this street past more quiet houses
until I reach an intersection with odd hanging lights—red,

green, yellow. Cars stop and go at it. And across the inter-section, I see buildings. Shops. At least I think they're shops; they're all so shiny. The sun seems to bounce off every-thing. I've never squinted this much in Gladder Hill, with or without my sun visor.

There's a sudden lull in the traffic—no cars—so I scurry across the intersection. People walk along the sidewalks, carrying bags or small children or both. Now I can see the shop signs a little better. One says Barkbee Pizza, to my relief. I'm still in Barkbee. I follow the sidewalk past Ringwold Pharmacy and Molly's Laundromat. Suddenly I notice movement in the corner of my right eye and turn to find someone walking beside me.

The mirror girl.

How is she everywhere?

Windows out here seem like second-rate mirrors: not as crisp and more confusing. They mix the mirror girl with stuff on the other side. In this case, people loading and emptying washing machines.

A small boy appears behind the window. He stares and points at me and says something I can't hear. A woman, maybe his mother, rushes over and glances at me before grabbing the boy's hand, tugging him away.

I turn from the shop window and walk on, trying to shake off the boy's stare. And I thought *I* had a staring problem.

But more people glance at me as I walk through the town. A man and a woman holding hands, a tall boy with spiky hair, a woman on a bike. I walk faster. Maybe everyone in this town has a staring problem.

I pass a bunch of restaurants: Grubby's Diner, the Horseshoe Restaurant and Bar, Fireside BBQ, Sunny Side Up Cafe... Jeez, people here have a lot more options than just the one we have in Gladder Hill, unless you count the school lunchroom or the ice cream stand at Wonderland. But the Gladder Hill Grill is only open on weekends, and Grandma's home-cooked meals usually taste better than Chef Jackson's—no offense to him.

As I pass a place called Becca's Bakery now, the scent of fresh bread makes my stomach growl. When was the last time I ate? It had to have been before the accident. Yesterday at school? And of course I have no money. All the more reason to find my mom; maybe she'll cook me something. And maybe her cooking will be just as good as Grandma's, or better.

*Don't think about Grandma.*

Granted, I have to be realistic about two things: First, just because people in Gladder Hill never move house—except Mr. Grinwold now—that doesn't mean people outside of Gladder

Hill don't either. My mom lived at 6 Creekside Road when I was born, but there's no guarantee she still does. If she doesn't, maybe whoever's living there can tell me where she moved to or how to find out. Maybe they'll even let me in for a minute so I can be someplace my mom once was. And use the bathroom.

Second, if she really abandoned me like Grandma said, there was obviously a reason. I just need to convince her she made a mistake. I'll need a strong argument. Something like:

**Top Reasons You Should Un-Abandon Me**
- I don't take up much space. All I need is a small room—I'll even sleep on the couch! I don't snore either (that I know of).
- I clean up after myself and help around the house. (Grandma can back this up.)
- I can be fun. I like board games and card games and am never (well, almost never) a sore loser.
- I'm your daughter.

I'll have to think of more reasons to add to the list. It's hard to give it my full concentration right now, with all these faces around. Face after face, passing me by foot or car or coming out of shops... I try to count them as I walk down the street, but it's too hard to keep track. The faces of Gladder Hill were only the tip of the iceberg. Noah's Pop Eyes would be out of their sockets right now.

Despite all these people, I'm alone. In a strange town. I remind myself that I chose this. And that soon I won't be alone.

There's just one thing keeping me from 6 Creekside Road: directions. I've never needed directions before. I've always known how to get everywhere in Gladder Hill, but then again, Gladder Hill *was* everywhere. It was my whole world. I'm not sure how to even go about getting directions here, aside from asking someone—which would draw more attention to me, and I'm trying to draw *less*.

I look around for a shop that might sell maps. Not that I've ever seen a map of anything other than Gladder Hill, but Barkbee must have its own map too. As I reach the end of Main Street, I spot a redbrick building with a bike rack that spells READ and big words above the front doors: BARKBEE PUBLIC LIBRARY. I perk up. In Gladder Hill, the library was the place to go for information, even if it didn't answer all my questions.

Here's hoping this library will answer at least one.

# 17

THE AUTOMATIC FRONT DOORS slide open for me, but not before the mirror girl flashes there. I can't seem to go three minutes without seeing her—she won't leave me alone.

It probably doesn't help that I keep looking for her.

Inside, I blink in the vastness of the space. I was expecting one room, like the Gladder Hill Library. But here bookshelves stretch on either side of me, and a staircase leads up to—I crane my neck—at least *two* more floors.

I walk past people sitting at tables. A few bend their heads over books, as I'd expect at a library, but some are moving their fingertips across devices that rest in the palms of their hands. Others are typing on odd-looking typewriters. The keyboards on these typewriters remind me of the electric typewriters we use in Gladder Hill, only instead of paper, these ones have a thin, flat rectangle extending up from them that people are looking at as they type. The devices seem to hold their users' full attention, which works in my favor: no one's staring at me.

The library has some of the same sections that Gladder Hill's has, only much bigger. Gardening, nature, cookbooks, children's literature... I pick up a random book from a shelf. *Anne of Green Gables* by L. M. Montgomery. A picture of a girl on the cover surprises me. A bright smile, red hair in two long tails, cheeks with light-brown specks—all rendered in a colorful drawing.

My stomach dances. Books like this would never be seen in Gladder Hill. Our books have some nonhuman illustrations inside, but the covers show nothing but the title and the author's name against solid colors. No pictures, let alone pictures of people. *Never judge a book by its cover*—I remember Principal Gladder hammering this phrase into us in interiority lessons. I always thought it was a weird thing to tell us when all our book covers look the same. But here in this library, the phrase makes more sense.

I find myself wanting to know more about this Anne girl. I turn the book over and read the blurb on the back. *Orphan Anne Shirley has always hated her red hair...* Another surprise. None of the books we have in Gladder Hill physically describe people. Ever. Most of them aren't even about people but rather animals or science or math. I don't have time to read the book now, but I already have so many questions. Why would Anne hate red hair? Is it something I should hate too?

My stomach growls again. I put the book back on the shelf and force myself to focus on the reason I'm in here. I scan the stacks for a map section. Maybe it's in a different part of the library. As I cross toward the stairs, I pass those tables with people reading or looking at their devices. One of the smaller handheld devices lies on a table, unattended. I pause and stare at it. What is it anyway? It's like nothing I've seen before.

Curiosity gets the better of me: I pick it up. A face moves on the object's dark-gray surface. I gasp. It's the mirror girl again but dimmer—vaguer. Is this thing a sort of mirror too?

When I touch the surface, it lights up, and the mirror girl vanishes. In her place appear today's date, the time, and an image of a black dog—as lifelike as the puppy in the picture from Grandma's room—above the words *enter passcode*.

"Hey! That's my phone!"

I jerk my head up. A tall boy is pointing and running toward me from a restroom across the room. "That kid is stealing my phone!"

Heads turn toward me. People whisper.

Stealing? I shake my head and open my mouth to explain, but the device slips from my sweaty hands and falls to the hard floor with a *thwack*.

"What the—you better not have cracked the screen, you freak!" The boy lunges forward, the veins in his neck bulging. I spin away from him. "Hey!" I hear him call, but I don't look back as I sprint through the front doors.

I bump into someone outside—"Watch it," they bark—but I don't have time to apologize. I keep running back down Main Street. I don't know where I'm going—back to the woods? Wherever that library boy can't find me. Pedestrians stare and step out of my way. *Freak*, the boy called me. What does it mean? And why was he calling that device a phone? It didn't look like one—at least not the ones we have back home. And the screen he was talking about... I've never seen a screen like that device, that rectangle. Then again, it showed me the mirror girl; no wonder we don't have it in Gladder Hill.

My nostrils tickle as I run. Uh-oh. I reach up, and my hand comes away bloody. Now is not the time for another nosebleed. It's probably gotten on my bandages. And this time I can't just go to the school nurse. I feel nauseous now too, my empty stomach twisting. Maybe I shouldn't have left the hospital. Maybe I should have let them take me back to Gladder Hill, where I at least know how the world works...

"Hey!"

And now the library boy has chased me down, or maybe even the police. I should just let them get me. Besides, I'm too dizzy to keep running. I stumble and lean against a brick wall—feel someone touch my elbow. "Hey, are you...?"

I look up into a face that confuses me. I can't see the person's eyes. In their place, I see not one, but *two* of the mirror girl, framed in a pair of dark ovals with a rainbowlike shine to them. They're attached in the middle and resting on the bridge of the person's nose. I can't see through them—I can only see the two mirror girls staring out at me...

Then the person pulls the object off her face, revealing actual eyes. Green ones, peering down at my shirt, toward the spot on my chest where it says, *Everyone's gladder in Gladder Hill.*

Her eyes widen. "Are you from Gladder Hill?" Something glints on her teeth as she talks.

And then I realize I've seen that face before. I've *drawn* that face before.

"Beryl?"

# 18

O H MY GOD...HAYLEY?" BERYL'S jaw drops.

"It's Zailey, but—"

Beryl smacks her forehead. "I knew that."

"You were close."

"Sorry—I couldn't tell it was you at first." Her eyes flit over my bandages. "But it had to be. You're the only kid from Gladder Hill who'd know my name. Are you okay?"

"I think so." I pinch my nose and try to ignore the people staring at me as they walk by. "Dang nosebleed."

"What the heck are you doing here?"

"Long story."

"Here." Beryl ushers me into an alleyway; she must notice the stares too. She pulls a mini pack of tissues out of her backpack.

"Thanks." I hold a tissue under my nostrils.

"I thought you couldn't leave Gladder Hill till you grow up," she says. "That's what the tour guide said."

"Well, I sort of escaped."

Her eyebrows rise. "Like, you ran away? All the way from Gladder Hill? That's at least an hour's drive."

"I got a ride part of the way." I don't want to get into the accident right now. Plus, another wave of nausea is crashing through me. My knees buckle.

"Whoa." Beryl catches me by the arm. "Come on. Let's go to my house."

"Really?"

"It's only a few minutes away." Beryl smiles and sets those dark ovals back in front of her eyes. "And my parents are still at work." Her cheerfulness is contagious, and I can't help feeling a little better. She guides me along, pointing out her favorite places—an ice cream parlor, a cinema (whatever that is), and a coffee shop on the corner. "My mom's their top customer," Beryl says. "She needs a lot of caffeine for her job."

"What does she do?"

"Oh, she's a sort of…journalist, you could say. Lots of deadlines."

"She keeps a journal?"

Beryl laughs. "Not exactly. Don't you have journalists in Gladder Hill?"

I think of the list of jobs in the college brochure. "Don't

think so." I sigh. "We have other jobs, but none that I want to do."

"What do you want to do?" She steers me onto a quieter street, Marigold Crescent.

"Well..." I glance sidelong at her. I've never told anyone what I really want to do. "I kind of want to be an artist," I say. "Like, a professional one. That would be cool."

"You could be one out here. Lots of people sell their stuff online."

"Online?" I imagine artists hanging their drawings and paintings on a line like laundry, but that doesn't seem right.

Beryl nods but doesn't explain, and now she's stopping in front of a house a lot like the ones on Peony Circle. "Here we are." She pulls a shiny object out of her backpack and inserts it into a slot in the front door, turns it, and then pushes the door open. Interesting. People don't use key cards out here?

"Need anything for your nose?" Beryl asks as I follow her into an entrance hall. "We have an ice pack in the freezer."

I lower the tissue from my nose. "No, thanks. I think the bleeding stopped. I do have to pee though."

"Bathroom's this way." She leads me up a staircase. So far, this could be the inside of a Gladder Hill house. It has a carpet, stairs, walls...

Then a face, hanging in a frame on the wall.

Nope, not a Gladder Hill house.

"Is that you?" I point. The image is crisp and clear, like Lydia's nurse badge and the picture I found in Grandma's room.

Beryl looks back at the picture and rolls her eyes. "Ugh, yeah, that's my school photo. I hate it."

"Photo?" My heart leaps. "Does that have anything to do with photography?"

She laughs. "Uh, it has everything to do with it."

I can't help smiling at this discovery. I was beginning to think *photography* wasn't a real word. So is this what my mom does at her photography studio? Create images like this?

"Here's the bathroom," Beryl says. "I'll be in my room— it's this door right across."

"Cool, thanks."

In the bathroom, the mirror girl flashes above the sink. I doubt I could ever get used to her popping up everywhere. She looks the same as the last time I saw her, except now a few trickles of blood are drying on the bandages below her nose. I try to wipe them off with my fingers, but that doesn't do much, so I turn on the sink. The basin is made of black marble, which surprises me. I don't think I've ever seen a black sink. In Gladder Hill they're all white or light-colored at the bottom, like our pots and bowls.

I cup some water in my hands to splash onto the bandages. Something's not right though. It's the way the water looks. Right away I can see through it to my palms. No extra air is being pumped into this water. Is it safe to use? To touch?

I part my hands and watch the black sink fill up faster than it can drain—probably because there's only one drain hole. Gladder Hill sinks are covered with them. Suddenly I see a figure wavering in the water.

I turn off the sink and squint. As the water stills, the figure crystallizes into the mirror girl.

My head spins. I watch the water drain and the mirror girl with it. I always thought our water in Gladder Hill was pumped with extra air for health and safety reasons. Granted, we've never been given much more explanation than that. And yet I never questioned it. No kids did.

But if water—pure water—can be a sort of mirror, then so many things in Gladder Hill make more sense now. Like why we have all those drain holes that rain and sink and shower water disappears into. And why Principal Gladder built Gladder Hill in such a dry area. And why we've been fed those vague "health and safety" reasons for clouding water and keeping liquids covered... Was there ever any truth to them?

I wipe my hands on a towel, trying to stay calm. One thing is especially clear: Principal Gladder has gone to a lot of trouble to keep reflections out of Gladder Hill.

Are they really that dangerous?

I guess nature creates plenty of things we should protect ourselves from, like droughts and storms. But reflections in water don't seem on the same level. Droughts and storms can kill you. Reflections can't. Can they? Maybe if you believe in the mirror demon...

"You okay in there?" Beryl calls through the door.

I jump. "Yep, be out in a minute."

I got so distracted that I forgot to pee. I do that now, wash my hands in the unclouded water, and then find Beryl sitting on her bed in the room across the hall.

"All good?" She glances up from a device in her hand. It looks like the so-called phone the boy in the library had.

"Yep," I say, trying to act as if I didn't just have a revelation about water. I look around. Beryl's bedroom is a cabinet of curiosities. Strange objects lie scattered on top of her dresser. I examine them, struggling to make sense of their labels: *Outshine lip gloss, LA Girl nail polish, Chic Pro hair straightener...* I lift the lid on a container labeled *loose shimmer powder for face & body* and pick up the puff-like thing that sits on top; the powder underneath looks like ground cinnamon, which I would never think to put on my face. I drop the puff back in place, but then a cloud of it explodes up onto my shirt.

I turn to Beryl and start apologizing, but she looks at my shirt and laughs. "Don't worry about it. It's no big deal. You can change into one of my shirts. They should fit. What size are you?"

"What do you mean?"

She frowns. "You know, what do the tags on your clothes say?"

I pull the back collar of my shirt over my shoulder and crane my neck to look at the tag. "One size fits all," I read.

"No wonder your shirt is so baggy." She pulls out a yellow garment and tosses it to me. "This tank top looks like it would fit you."

She turns away as I change into the strangely named *tank top.* "Interesting," I mutter, peering down. It exposes my shoulders and hugs my skin. The slight bumps in my chest are even more obvious now. I fidget with the bottom hem. "It feels kind of tight."

"It's supposed to be tight. See, it looks good on you."
Beryl points to a long rectangle on her closet door. The mirror
girl flashes there, and this time I can see all of her at once—
not just her head but everything below the Uncrossable
Boundary. Stuff I could always see, just from a different
perspective—her legs, her arms, her middle...

"What's the matter?" Beryl says. I watch a reverse
image of Beryl next to the mirror girl, turning her head.
Mirror Beryl looks right at me. Her hand flies to her mouth.
"Wait. Oh my god. Today's your first time seeing your
reflection, isn't it?"

I shrug, as if it's not something I'd been anticipating for
years.

"Whoa," she breathes. "This must be so weird for you.
I mean, I know you have the bandages on, but still... Is it
weird to see yourself?"

"A little," I say—the understatement of the year.

Mirror Beryl nods, still looking at me. I turn my head
to look at actual Beryl; *she's* looking away from me, toward
the mirror. When I glance back at the mirror, Mirror
Beryl's gaze is still on me. She raises an eyebrow. "What's
wrong?"

"It's just..." I shake my head. "Mirrors are bizarre."

"Is that why you ran away?" Mirror Beryl cocks her head. "To see your reflection?"

"No," I snap. Then I realize how defensive I sound and clear my throat. "I'm going to see my mom. She lives here in Barkbee."

"Really? Why doesn't she live in Gladder Hill with you?"

"That's what I'm going to find out."

"Oh. And she knows you're coming?"

"Yep." I look away from Mirror Beryl. I don't know why I've lied. Maybe I don't want Beryl to judge my plan—to try to spoil it. So what if I'm going to surprise my mom? Aren't surprises more fun?

Of course, there's a part of me—a tiny part—that doesn't want to call or write to my mom first, in case she tells me not to come. If I show up unannounced, she'll have no choice but to see me and take me in. My own mother wouldn't turn me away, right?

I just need directions.

My belly roars.

And maybe something to eat.

Beryl's eyes widen. "I think we need to feed that lion in your stomach."

"I won't say no to that."

She grins and gets to her feet. "We can even watch TV while we eat, since my parents aren't home."

"TV?"

Beryl puffs out her cheeks. "I have so much to teach you."

# 19

THERE'S SOMETHING CALLED *DISNEY* out here in the real world. Apparently it's a big deal. I sit on Beryl's couch, looking through her collection of Disney "movies": colorful cases illustrated with drawings of women and labeled with strange titles. *The Little Mermaid... Beauty and the Beast... Cinderella... Frozen...*

"Are there people who look like this?" I call into the kitchen, where Beryl is microwaving macaroni and cheese.

"Kind of," she calls back. "I mean, the people who play them at Disney World *almost* look like them. But not everyone's that lucky."

*Lucky.* I stare at the women on the cases: plain faces with small noses, pink lips, big eyes, long lashes... Hardly any details or shading like the drawings in my collection. So this look is considered lucky? I wonder what's considered unlucky.

"Here you go." Beryl places my drink on a coaster on the

coffee table—water in a weird cup: see-through like Barkbee windows and open at the top like that cup at the hospital.

My first instinct is not to drink from it, despite my thirst.

Then Beryl takes a sip from her own uncovered drink. I think of the bathroom sink upstairs. And the possibility—no, the near certainty—that adults in Gladder Hill have been lying to me my whole life about liquids. I drank the uncovered water at the hospital, and I'm fine.

My jaw tightens. I pick up the cup and take a big sip. *Take that, Principal Gladder. Take that, Grandma.*

Beryl pops back into the kitchen and returns with a bowl of macaroni and cheese and a spoon, setting them in front of me.

"Mmm, thank you." I pick up the spoon; it's shinier than any spoon I've seen in Gladder Hill. I turn it over, examining it. A face on the back startles me.

"Oh, is it dirty?" Beryl points at the spoon. "I can get you another one."

"No. It's good." I smile and scoop up some macaroni, trying to act normal. So it's true: a spoon can be a mirror. At this point nothing should surprise me. I try to picture Mr. Grinwold alone in his house, holding a spoon like this, looking at its surface. Why did he stay in Gladder Hill if he wanted to break the rules? He's an adult; no one was holding him prisoner there.

Or is it not as simple as that?

"I'll just flip through the channels," Beryl says as she joins me on the couch. "Let me know if you see anything you want to watch."

I still can't get over this whole TV thing. I had to ask Beryl to explain three times how it works—how people get on the screen—and I'm still not sure I understand. But one thing's clear enough: I can see hundreds of faces just in this rectangle attached to the wall. I don't even have to go outside. And *they* can't see *me,* so I can stare all I want.

The screen morphs now into a bunch of women playing soccer.

"Uh-oh, France is winning," Beryl says.

"Who's France?"

She laughs. "No, France the country. The US needs to beat them to make it to the World Cup."

Country? Teachers have only ever mentioned one country: America, the one we're in. My mind races. Now that I think about it, they've never said it's the only country. They've just never suggested otherwise. My stomach turns. Was this one of their attempts to keep us uninterested in what's outside the gates? The less that we think is out there, the less reason we'll have to want to leave...

"Oh, right, France," I mumble, not wanting Beryl to know how they tricked me.

One of the players kicks the ball, and it smacks another player in the jaw. Beryl winces. "Good thing she's wearing a mouth guard."

"Yeah," I say, glad to change the subject. "I have to wear one for Ultimate Frisbee. I hate the way it tastes though."

"Oh, I'd wear one all the time if I had an excuse," Beryl says. "It hides my braces." Her voice flattens. "My metal mouth, as Ross Bradhurst calls it at school." She prods one of the glinting squares on her teeth with her finger.

*Those* are braces? I've heard of them—a pamphlet in the dentist's office back home explains how you can get them on the back or front of your teeth "if necessary" for health reasons— but I've never seen any Gladder Hill residents wearing them.

"At least they'll make your teeth healthier, right?" I say, scooping up another mouthful of macaroni and cheese.

Beryl shrugs. "My mom says it will be worth it when my teeth are perfectly straight." She sighs and changes the channel to some woman singing in a sunflower field. "I should just suck it up. Millions of people wear braces."

I pause midchew and stare at her. "Mill...millions?"

She gestures at the TV. "Well, unless you're a celeb—then you get veneers. My mom's researched it for work."

I don't know what a *celeb* or *veneers* are, but I'm still processing what she said before that. My heart pumps faster. "Are there...millions of people in the world?"

Beryl frowns at me. "Well, yeah. More than that. Isn't the world population, like, seven billion?"

I almost choke on my mac and cheese.

"Jeez, they don't teach you much in Gladder Hill, do they?"

As she flips through more channels, I try to wrap my head around this new information. Even Noah's guess of thousands of faces seemed unfathomable to me. But billions? I wish I could tell Noah—he'd never believe me.

"Are they all different?" I murmur. "All seven billion faces?"

Beryl tilts her head. "Well, there are identical twins. Like my cousins. But even they don't look *exactly* the same."

*Identical twins?* I'm about to ask for details when someone on the TV catches my eye.

But Beryl changes the channel before I can get a good look.

"Wait," I say. "Can you go back?"

She flips back. "This?"

There she is: a young woman walking down a stair-case in a long blue garment that shimmers like I've never seen clothes shimmer. I've never seen a face shimmer like that either. Her skin sort of glows. Black stuff outlines her eyes. Her lips are dark red, her teeth extra white. Yellowish hair balances in a pile on top of her head, with some strands hanging in front.

"Oh, right." Beryl laughs. "This is that cheesy prom rom-com my mom loves."

"I feel like I've seen that woman before." I watch the young woman stop at the foot of the stairs, where a young man waits for her. "But I can't…" I squint as the woman holds out her hand, and the man slides some sort of flower on a loop onto her wrist. She gazes up at him through long lashes, and I study her face: speckless, spotless, dotless, a little boring…

Wait a minute.

Beryl nods. "You sure have. Say hello to your principal."

# 20

WHAT?" I BLINK AT the TV screen. "Principal Gladder?"

It can't be her. This face isn't as round as the face I know. It has more dips, more hollows, more places where I'd have to put shading if I were to draw her again. And her arms—they're like sticks. And her middle—it's almost as narrow as her head.

And yet...

"So should we go to this prom thing or what?" the guy says to the young woman.

"As long as I get to see you dance, I don't care where we go." She smirks, and though her voice sounds young, there's something familiar about it—and that smirk. And as I stare at the screen, I glimpse her in there: unmistakable bits of Principal Gladder. The shape of her nose, the size of her forehead, the intensity of her eyes...

"Yep," Beryl says. "That's her, fifteen years ago or

whenever this was filmed. A lo-o-o-ong time ago anyway. She was in a ton of teen movies."

The screen darkens and then shows a guy squeezing toothpaste onto a toothbrush. "Ever wish your teeth were whiter?" says a voice. Beryl flips the channel, but the image of the young woman still hovers before me.

"She looked so different," I murmur, feeling a wave of guilt. Like I've invaded Principal Gladder's privacy by glimpsing this other part of her life—even though anyone outside Gladder Hill can apparently see her like this on their TVs.

"Really?" Beryl turns to me. "What does she look like now? No one has seen her since she moved to Gladder Hill. That place is paparazzi-proof, or so my mom says. And she didn't come out when I was there for the school trip."

"Well, she's..." I close my eyes, trying to conjure Principal Gladder—to separate her from the woman on the TV. Then I realize it would be easier if I just draw her. "Do you have a pencil and a blank piece of paper?" I ask.

She finds what I need in a drawer. I kneel on the floor, with the paper on the coffee table, and then I transport the face that lives in my mind onto the page, one pencil stroke at a time.

Beryl hovers over me, watching. "Whoa...you can really draw. I can barely do stick figures."

I don't know what she means by stick figures, but I keep going so I don't lose my concentration. When I finish, I hand Beryl the drawing.

"Wow, you're right—she does look different," Beryl says. "Can I keep this? It's so cool that you can draw like this."

I can't help feeling flattered. Is it really that good? "Sure," I say. I'm not in Gladder Hill, after all; I don't have to worry about getting in trouble for drawing anymore.

She smiles, holding up the drawing like it's some sort of masterpiece. "Even Nancy Bradley can't draw this good. She's this girl in my art class who thinks she's all that. I wish you went to my school so you could show her up."

"Well...maybe soon I will."

"Really?" She turns to me, her smile widening.

"If my mom lets me stay with her—" I stop short. My mom—the reason I'm here in the first place. "Wait, what time is it?"

Beryl checks her phone. "Wow, almost five already."

I shouldn't have let it get so late. "Do you have a map of Barkbee?" I ask.

"Like, Google Maps? Yeah, here." Beryl hands me her phone. "Just make sure the Wi-Fi's on."

I stare at all the icons on the screen. "What's Wi-Fi?"

Her eyebrows rise. "Oh boy."

After Beryl tries to explain the "internet" and answers my deluge of questions—"Wait, what's a Google?" and "Hold on, you can ask it *anything*?"—she helps me look up directions to 6 Creekside Road.

"Oh, I see. It's at the other end of Barkbee." She points at the map on the screen. "You'll need a ride. I can ask one of my parents to take you when they get home if you want?"

I chew my lip. "It's already getting late. Can't I just walk?"

"It'd take a half hour. You can catch a bus part of the way though."

"A bus? I've never taken a bus."

"There's a stop one block over. It only costs a buck each way. Do you have any money with you?"

I shake my head. "I think I'll just walk."

Beryl reaches into her pocket and pulls out a greenish slip of paper. "Just use this. It's left over from my school lunch." She hands me the paper. I stare at the face in the center of it, a man with funny white hair and a straight mouth; the name *Washington* arches in a ribbon underneath.

"You look like you've never seen a dollar bill before," Beryl says.

"Ours don't look like this."

She frowns. "You guys don't use dollars?"

"We do. They just don't have faces on them."

"Wow." She shakes her head. "That's hard-core."

"I don't want to take your money." I try to hand the bill back to her.

"Keep it." She waves it away and continues channel surfing. "If you don't want it for the bus, consider it payment for your drawing. There, now you can call yourself a professional artist."

I like the sound of that. I thank her and glance back at Washington. He looks a bit like Mr. Aberdeen, Gladder Hill's golf cart taxi driver. I slip him in my pocket and put on my sneakers.

"Um...Zailey?"

"Yeah?" I tighten my laces.

"There's something you should see."

I look up. A woman on the TV screen is sitting at a desk, saying something about a search party, an escaped patient. A banner below her stops my heart:

12-YEAR-OLD GLADDER HILL RESIDENT MISSING

# 21

BERYL TURNS UP THE volume.

"Zailey was last seen at Sunrise Children's Hospital today around three fifteen," the commentator is saying. "Several people have now reported seeing someone who fits her description about a half hour later in downtown Barkbee and the Barkbee Public Library, but there have been no sightings since then."

"Oh my god," Beryl murmurs. I'm frozen to the couch, unable to tear my gaze away from this stranger who's talking about me in a rectangle on the wall. Is this real life?

"Bandages cover most of Zailey's face, and she's believed to be wearing drawstring linen pants and a T-shirt that says, *Everyone's gladder in Gladder Hill*. We're not able to show a photo of Zailey, as none exist, but if you think you've seen anyone matching this description, please call the number below…"

Beryl perches on the edge of the couch, biting her

lip. "Yikes. This is a big deal. It sounds like they're really worried." She turns to me. "Maybe you should tell them you're okay."

"No. No way."

"You could pretend you got lost. I'm sure they won't be mad."

"No," I repeat, louder than I mean to.

Beryl shrinks back.

"Sorry, I just—you don't get it." I stand and start pacing the room. "My grandma's the reason I'm wearing these bandages."

"What?" Beryl's eyes widen.

I realize she's been too polite to ask about my bandages and why I'm wearing them. Maybe now's the time to tell her. I take a deep breath and explain what happened—how Grandma found my drawings and threw them in the greasy pot and set them on fire right in front of me.

Beryl's jaw drops. "How could she put you in danger like that—her own grandkid?"

I may have exaggerated about how close the pot was to me—I may have left out the part where I ran across the kitchen to get to it and lifted the lid—but I need to make Beryl understand that I can't go back to Grandma. And it feels good to tell someone what happened and not have it just live in my head.

"And now she wants to keep me in Gladder Hill forever," I say. "And keep me from drawing, and from seeing my mom, and I just…" I look at Beryl. "Do you get it now? Why I ran away?"

"I guess so."

"So will you promise not to tell anyone you saw me or know where I'm going?" I clasp my hands together. "Please?"

Beryl hesitates. I must look desperate enough, because she finally nods. "Okay. I promise."

I breathe out.

"I guess I wouldn't want to go back either if I were you."

"Thank you."

She smiles. "That's what friends are for."

"We're friends?"

"Aren't we?"

I grin. "I don't see why not."

"But *you* have to promise *me* something," she says.

"What?"

"That you'll let me know how it goes with your mom. Here's my phone number." She grabs a pen from the table, lifts my hand, and jots some digits on my palm.

"Deal."

The commentator on the TV screen is talking now about "soaring gas prices," which makes Beryl yawn and turn the TV off.

"I'd better get going," I say. "Do you have something I could write these directions on?" I hold up her phone with its Google Maps.

"Besides your hand?" She laughs. "We can just print them upstairs. That's faster."

She gets up and leads me out of the living room. As we pass the front door to get to the stairs, I hear something jangling outside. Beryl and I freeze. "That's my mom," she whispers. "Quick, go hide in my room. Close the door and don't make a sound, okay? I'll come up as soon as I get her off my back."

Before I can say anything, the door starts to open. Beryl shoos me away. I dash up the stairs.

"Hey, Mom," I hear Beryl say. "How was your day?"

"Wow, someone's cheerful," a woman's voice responds. "Is that a crime?"

I tiptoe into Beryl's room and shut the door as slowly and quietly as I can. I listen to the muffled tones below me, but I can't make out what they're saying now.

I still have Beryl's phone in my hand, so I set it on the bed. Now what? I look around. I have no idea how Beryl was planning to "print" the directions; I don't see any sort of typewriter to type them up. I'd better just write them down like I planned. I pull up the directions and the map on Beryl's phone and look them over again before I get some paper from Beryl's desk. But I can't find anything to write with. I scan her stuff, peering into the cubbyholes under the desk. Binders, books, a crinkled leaflet.

### Life in Gladder Hill: Mission and Policies

I recognize that title—it's the leaflet Beryl dropped during the tour. I can't resist picking it up again now.

### Introduction

Welcome to Gladder Hill, a safe space where residents live free from physical ideals and concerns about their appearance. Here, adults already exposed to such influences can heal, and young children can uniquely develop without them…

That's nothing new to me, though it's weird to see it

written out so formally. I skip ahead, past the sections on the founding story, the dress code, and banned materials and items.

Precautions Regarding Water and Other Liquids

Here I slow down.

…several measures in place to diminish mirrorlike properties in liquids. For example, the water supply is pumped with extra oxygen…

I skim the section.

…pots, bowls, and other receptacles must have light-colored interiors…coffee cannot be drunk black and is only available as a premix…all beverages are consumed through closed, spill-proof containers…

It doesn't mention anything about the health and safety explanations we've been fed.

A niggling feeling builds up inside me, one that's been there since I saw the water in Beryl's sink. What else have adults lied to us about?

Media and Language Restrictions

Here the word *dictionaries* catches my eye.

...and therefore, 107 words and their derivatives have either been omitted entirely from our dictionaries or amended to omit certain definitions and usages. These words include:

- attractive
- beautiful
- chubby
- cute
- fat
- good-looking
- gorgeous
- handsome
- hideous
- overweight
- petite
- plump
- pretty
- thin
- scrawny
- skinny
- slender
- ugly
- unattractive
- underweight

The list keeps going. I stare at it: a whole inventory of words I've never heard. Except for one. *Cute.* Beryl said that once. So it isn't local lingo? It's a normal English word that's been deliberately hidden from us? The niggling feeling sharpens into a sting of betrayal. I grab Beryl's phone and do a keyword search on Google like she showed me. *Definition of cute*, I type.

*adjective*

> *having a pleasing and usually endearing appearance*
>
> *"She had a cute little nose."*

Of course. The word has to do with appearance. Maybe all these words do. My eyes linger on the second word, *beautiful. Beau...*

Hold on.

*It's a beau—er, a nice day out.*

*Oh, that's beau—uh, lovely.*

Could that be the word Mr. Mackafee and Grandma almost said those times?

I start to look up *beautiful*, but then Beryl's phone vibrates, and I jump, dropping it on the floor.

I wince as it thuds and vibrates there for a few more seconds. Did Beryl and her mom hear that downstairs?

Either way, I should get out of here. Beryl is taking too long—and what am I waiting for anyway? I put the leaflet back where I found it. It would be nice to look over the directions to my mom's house one more time, but I'm worried the phone will start vibrating again. And I can picture the map in my head—I guess that's one benefit of my "eidetic memory" or whatever Mr. Huttle called it. The route didn't seem complicated.

Beryl's room has two windows. One looks out on the street: not ideal for staying out of sight. Beryl mentioned a bus stop across the street, but if I'm on the news...if people are looking for me...the bandages will give me away. That was one thing the news commentator had mentioned. Good thing I at least changed out of my Gladder Hill T-shirt.

I go to the other window, which looks out on a backyard and trees. Those woods would keep me out of sight. And according to the map, I can cut through them. Beryl said it was only a half-hour walk to my mom's house, and that's without the shortcut. I walk twice that much most days in Gladder Hill—that's nothing.

So I leave Beryl's dollar on her bed and open the back window. I wish I could say goodbye or leave her a thank-you note—why doesn't she have anything to write with in here?—but I hope she'll understand why I had to go.

As I hoist my leg up over the sill, I feel like I'm having déjà vu. Didn't I already escape out a window today? I look down and gulp. This time I'm a floor farther from the ground. I hover on the window ledge before taking a deep breath and clambering down the drainpipe. I tumble into a flower bed—*ouch*. Luckily the window I fell in front of has the curtains drawn.

I scramble to my feet and slip into the woods for the second time today. I just hope I'm going the right way.

# 22

THE HEAT CAN BE harsh enough in normal conditions. When bandages are smothering your face, it's ten times harsher. The woods at least offer some shade—that is, until I reach the end of them.

Beyond the woods lies a quiet, open road; this must be the road that leads to my mom's street. There's no other way to go from here.

My heart starts to drum. No more woods—no more concealment. I reach up and touch my bandages. Anyone who spots me with these on will know who I am if they've seen the news. Nurse Lydia said I should keep them on to prevent infection and irritation, but maybe she was being dramatic. Besides, wouldn't it be good to let some air on my cheeks—to let my skin breathe?

I've made up my mind. I start at the bottom, just under my chin, tugging gingerly. The bandages resist at first, but once I tear and peel back the edges, the rest comes off freely.

After I pull away the last bit, I fold up the bandages and stuff them in my pockets until I can find a trash bin. I wait for the cool relief of air on my face, the sudden exposure of my pores, but the feeling isn't as noticeable as I expected. It must be that hot out.

I blink as dark spots speckle the outer edge of my vision in my left eye, the one that had been covered. They don't go away even after I blink a few more times. Maybe my eye just needs to adjust after being covered for so long. I try not to dwell on it as I head down the road. I also try to keep my hands at my sides, but my fingertips seem to have other plans. There's no stopping them—up they go, touching, feeling above the Uncrossable Boundary, searching for the familiar textures, the surface they know so well.

But they're met with new terrain. Some parts feel squishy. Blistered. Other parts feel dry. Leathery. I could be feeling a stranger's face, for all I know. No, I *am* feeling a stranger's face. Because this one isn't mine.

My heart clenches. I know I got burned, but I thought my fingers would still recognize what's up there. The skin would be a bit rough, maybe, but still the skin my fingertips knew.

I even expected it to feel sore—sorer than it actually does. The squishy parts hurt, but when I touch the leathery parts, I feel nothing. Not that I want to be sore, but considering the pain I felt when it happened, shouldn't the burns hurt more?

Then I remember something I overheard the doctor say to Grandma. *There may be some nerve damage.*

The dread in my stomach rises. I don't want this awareness. I just want to go back now, back to before I removed the bandages.

But I can't. All I can do is focus on finding my mom.

The sun sits low in the sky. Her house shouldn't be far, but who knows if I'll get lost or run into obstacles? I need to pick up the pace.

At least this road is quiet. The houses on them are quiet too—everyone must be away or inside in the AC. Now and then, I glimpse bluish-gray stuff sparkling in the sun beyond the houses. I can hear rushing water too. That must be what a creek looks and sounds like up close. I crane my neck over someone's fence and spot a little boat out on the water, moving down the creek. But then the rower looks up, so I hurry on.

I continue like this for a bit, trying not to touch my face again. Or worry about the dark spots still shrouding part of my vision in my left eye. Or think about how thirsty I am as the road slopes upward. I should have brought a bottle of water; I'm definitely learning all kinds of lessons about running away.

All of a sudden, the road curves to the left, and there it is: a green sign that says CREEKSIDE ROAD. My stomach somersaults. I'm finally on *the* road.

Houses line the left side, and bushes and trees line the other. The houses must be really spread out, because I only see one so far, in the distance. My heart drums as I walk toward it. It's big—the kind of house you'd never find in Gladder Hill because tall glass windows line the first floor. A woman is sitting behind one of the windows, her back to me. My heart drums faster and louder.

But as I approach the mailbox at the end of the driveway, I see the number: thirteen. A dog yaps at me from behind a fence. I hurry on.

It's about a minute's walk between each house. Number twelve, eleven, ten... I pant in the heat. I'm not used to a world that goes on and on with no gates to tell me to turn around. Number nine, eight, seven... As the numbers get lower and my pulse quickens, I go over my list in my head again: *Top Reasons You Should Un-Abandon Me: I don't take up much space; I clean up after myself; I can be fun; I'm your daughter...* I even think of a fifth one to add, now that I know about photography: *I'm artistic like you. I like drawing, and you like photography. I might like it too if you teach me. I can teach you to draw, if you don't already know how...*

As I walk, more woods appear instead of houses. Did I miss it? Where are the rest of the houses? The trees keep lining the road on both sides for at least five minutes, and just as my panic rises, the trees clear again and, at a dead end, the next house finally appears.

Or what used to be a house. The dark windows are smashed in. Vegetation grows into and out of them. The grass stands almost as tall as the fence. A candy wrapper flaps in the wind, caught in the hinge of the open front door. Spray-painted graffiti tarnishes the outside walls:

LIZZIE LOVES GRAHAM.
HAUNTED HOUSE—ENTER IF YOU DARE.
NATHAN IS A BUTTMUNCH.

The house must have been nice once, but the rusted front gate and moss-eaten birdbath suggest that was long ago. No lived-in house looks like this. I walk up to the front gate. My heart sinks. The number six is right there on the tilting mailbox.

6 Creekside Road.

My eyes burn with tears. This was my only hope. This was where my mom was supposed to be. This was where an exciting new life was supposed to be.

Nothing in the outside world has ended up as I imagined.

The sound of tires on gravel startles me. A motor whirring. I push open the rusty gate—it squeals—and run up the path to the house, weeds tickling my ankles.

I huddle in the entranceway behind the door and peer through the crack at the hinges. A car labeled BARKBEE POLICE comes around the bend and stops in front of the house. The car's front doors open, and two officers step out. I can hear a dog barking inside the car.

"You sure this is right?" the shorter one says, squinting at the house.

"It's the address he gave Jenkins," says the taller man. I can't see either of their faces too well, especially with the spots in my left eye, but I can just about hear them.

"Who did?"

"The girl's friend in Gladder Hill. He thinks she could be looking for her mom here—the address on her birth certificate."

My jaw tightens. Noah. How could he rat me out? I

thought he was on my side. Maybe he's jealous—jealous that I got out of Gladder Hill.

"This doesn't seem like the kind of place you'd find a twelve-year-old girl. Or anyone. Looks deserted."

"Well, it's the only lead we have right now. We should check inside anyway."

"Seems pointless, but okay. I'll get the dog out."

The shorter officer reaches for the back door of the car; I hear another bark. I'm toast.

Something buzzes. "Hang on." He raises a device to his mouth. "Yello, Sergeant Jeffrey here." A pause. "Ah." Another pause. "Got it. We're on our way."

"What now?"

"We've got her."

"Where?"

"Apparently she's at the Joneses' house, in their daughter's room. Doesn't know we're coming, so get in intervention mode."

"This should be interesting."

The men get back in the car and drive away.

The Joneses? That must be Beryl's house.

She must think I'm still in her room. She must not have come upstairs yet this whole time. For all she knows, I'm still hiding in there, waiting for her.

I feel the fresh sting of another betrayal. Beryl promised me. I imagine her talking to her mom, trying to act normal, until her mom mentions there's a missing girl in town—and then Beryl, probably a bad liar, caves and tells her I'm up in her room. I imagine them talking in whispers then, planning to call the police and have them capture me—because I certainly wouldn't go to the police willingly.

On the flip side, her betrayal is creating a diversion—buying me more time to find my mom.

I crouch there for a few minutes, watching through the crack in the door to make sure the police officers don't come back. No cars pass. No sounds. Just the silence of the house. I notice a spider crawling over my sneaker. I stand and shake it off. Everything is still.

I knock on the broken door, even though I've already entered. "Hello?" I call pointlessly. It's obvious I'm not going to get an answer. I knock again, harder, or maybe I'm just banging out of frustration. I ran away to find my mom, and if she doesn't live here anymore, what am I supposed to do now? I've put too much weight on this address, on assuming *someone*, if not my mom, would be here to at least tell me where she went.

But maybe there's some sign of her inside, some hint of where she moved to. It would be a waste not to check.

I take a few more steps into the house. It's dim in here. I try the light switch near me, flicking it once, twice— nothing. Of course, no one's paying the electric bill. I squint and distinguish the shape of a hallway. A staircase.

Something rustles; I jump. A mouse squeaks and scurries past me down the hall. I follow it, the floor creaking under me. The first room I come to is a sort of dining room. Or was. There's a table with half a dozen chairs, some tipped over, all of them strung with cobwebs. Broken chinaware covers the tablecloth. More graffiti marks the walls.

PETER WAS HERE.

JENNY K SMELLS!

IF YOU COULD HAVE ONE SUPERPOWER, WHAT WOULD IT BE?

I've never seen abandoned property before; every home in Gladder Hill is occupied. Clearly no one wants to occupy this one. Is my mom the one who left it like this? Why would she do that? It seems like a waste—a house still standing and no one using it. I walk through the dining room to what must have been a kitchen. A frying pan and a fork lie on the floor, among leaves and dirt that must have blown in through the smashed window, and the stove is growing stuff. The stove...

My stomach turns.

It's just a stove, just a kitchen. But then—that flash of orange, that blast of heat, the flames engulfing my face, my world....

I whirl away. For a second I think I'm going to be sick. I clutch my stomach and swallow the feeling, trying to swallow the memory too—that moment before the world went black. I breathe in and out and remind myself that the fire is extinguished. I'm fine. I'm okay.

Maybe I shouldn't have come here. I hurry back down the hall. I ought to leave anyway; there's clearly nothing to see in this house.

But where will I go? I hover in the doorway. My plan relied on my mom, or at least someone, being here. My stomach twists again at the thought of going back outside, turning myself in to the police, surrendering to my failed escape attempt.

Something rubs against my leg. I shriek, but it's not a mouse this time. An orange-and-white cat looks up at me, meowing.

I kneel and stroke his head. He reminds me of Tutu the calico from Gladder Hill, only without any black in his fur. His meows soften to purrs. I smile. There can't be anything too bad about this house if a cat wants to live in it. Cats are picky.

The cat yawns and wanders up the stairs. I follow, reaching out to put my hand on the railing. I stop just in time: dust coats it.

At the top of the staircase, I can go left or right. The cat goes right, so I do too. I follow him into what must have been a study. Books and pens lie scattered about the desk and the floor. Papers quiver in the wind that blows through the broken window. An armchair lies on its side. Moth-eaten curtains droop from a lopsided curtain rung.

The cat wanders into the next room.

The window in this room is smashed, but through a hole, I see a backyard: a swing set, a peach tree, and a slope of tall grass, all surrounded by a light-blue fence.

I've seen this backyard before.

Only there's no puppy, and now the swing set is rusted, the grass overgrown, the fence door closed, the paint peeling. My heart feels about to burst. My mom took that photograph here. At this house, her house.

But where did she move to? I turn and walk on through the room, still hoping to find a hint somewhere. The floor whines as I move across it and survey the area: The yellowing bed. The tipped-over nightstand. The dresser with the drawers pulled out and empty. The open doorway beyond, perhaps a bathroom, with a wooden threshold and octagonal floor tiles.

I pause, squinting.

White octagons outlined with orange, and inside each, orange and yellow petals and black flourishes...

My heart stops.

And then I'm seeing them both at the same time: the tiles in front of me, and my memory of them.

But as the memory flashes through my mind, there's something more this time, more than just floor tiles.

*Momma?*

A voice...a child's. A dog barking in the background.

The air hangs hot and heavy. Something happened in this room. Something terrible.

I blink, and there's a hand resting on the tile, limp, fingers curled, the rest of the arm out of view behind the doorframe.

I blink again, and the hand is gone. But the missing pieces of the memory snap into place, and all at once, I know. Someone died in this house. Not just someone. My mom.

And I was here when it happened.

I raise my hand to my mouth, stifling a cry. At the same

time, something moves in the room, in the corner of my eye. I jump and swivel to find someone staring at me: a face on the wall, hovering behind a cracked and filthy sheet of glass. But only for a second, before the floor groans—sags—crumbles beneath my feet.

# 23

M*EOW.*

A warm tongue licks my eyelids. Soft fur rubs against my cheek. It feels nice. But something else doesn't. No, not just something else. Everything else. My body, my legs, my arms. All of it feels twisted.

I blink, trying to open my eyes. Darkness lightens to dimness. Shapes, objects...fragments of wood, rubble, all around me. A hole in the ceiling above me.

I think I'm lying on my side. I try to sit up, but even moving my arm makes me wince. I try to wiggle my feet next, but I can't tell if they're doing as I bid them.

I open my mouth—at least I can do that. "Help," I call out. A scraggly croak emerges. Who is going to hear me when I sound like that? I try again. The cat's ears flatten, and he backs away. That's better.

I wait for someone to come.

Then I remember how far apart the houses on this street

are. And the police have already been here. What if they don't come back?

I squint at the phone number Beryl wrote on my hand; it blurs. And there's no working phone here, no electricity…

Maybe I'm getting what I deserve. I had Superficial thoughts. I drew faces, ran away, looked in mirrors. Let's face it: my mom was only part of the reason I ran away. I wanted to know her, but I also wanted to know what I looked like. I had it in my head that I could never completely know who I was until I knew that. And here I am, knowing only what I already knew: I'm Superficial. And Superficiality gets punished. I deserve to be punished. Am I in the otherworld from the children's tale now? Did the demon pull me through to the other side?

A new memory flashes before me: a blurred face in a dirty, broken mirror. Right before I fell. It was so quick, barely a glimpse. My mind has trouble conjuring it. But I remember the feeling it gave me, like the one I got from that bad dream about the tiles. Was it the mirror demon?

*Meow.*

A pink nose hovers in front of me, sniffing.

Why would the cat be in the demon's otherworld? And the sun…there's a sunbeam on my thigh.

But if I'm not in the otherworld, maybe I'd rather be, if it would make all this throbbing and stinging and aching go away. Pain in my arm. Pain in my leg. Pain in my face. Tears blur whichever world I'm in. I could let the pain take over; that almost seems easiest.

The cat and the rubble fade in and out of focus. Faces too. Olive's heart-shaped one. Noah's Pop Eyes. Beryl's cheek dent.

Grandma's pointy chin. Her creases and lines. Hazel eyes squinting as she smiles—as she reads—as she does a word search puzzle. I realize that these parts of her could look like anything, be swapped with anything, and they would still come to me now, because they're Grandma's. Is that why humans have faces in the end? So we can see them—the people we care about—before we die? So they can be with us, in a way, in those final moments?

Are these my final moments?

I can't remember the last thing I said to Grandma. It wasn't *I love you*. It wasn't anything nice. I was mad at her, but that's not what I think of now. Instead, I think of her omelets, her word search puzzles, her purple paradise. The way she calls me *kiddo*. And something she said once. *I could live without my sight...* In a flash I see her: alone, squinting, shuffling through a dim hallway, stretching out her arms, feeling her way. No contact lenses. She stumbles, trips, falls…

I try to sit up again—*ouch.*

*I could live without my sight. It's you I couldn't live without.*

She already lost a daughter. I don't know how it happened, but I know it happened in this house. If she loses me too…

I can't do that to her. I can't leave her all alone.

I listen to my heart thumping in my chest. Saving myself would require standing, and walking, but how can I do that when I can't even sit up? I try to think of happy things, other reasons to make myself move. Ice cream, colored pencils, Wonderland, Noah's laugh. My mom's photograph—the swing set, the peach tree, the fence, all of it footsteps away from me now, if I could just get up. She must have taken that photograph years ago, and yet, what I saw out the window today almost matched. The only missing parts were the puppy and the wheelbarrow. And the little wooden boat and the water beyond it, because the fence door was closed…

The boat.

I blink at the sunbeam on my thigh. Yes, there was a

boat in the picture, like the boat I saw on the way here, float-ing out on the water, moving down the creek.

I wriggle onto my back. Could my mom's boat still be out there, hidden behind the fence?

The cat meows again, placing a paw on my arm. Somehow that's my wake-up call; I push through the pain and pull myself into a sitting position, wincing while debris tumbles off me onto the floor. Spots flicker around my vision, especially my left eye. My head throbs. I cradle my right arm, which aches and stings with scrapes. I move my left leg. My right one takes more effort and—*ow, ow, ow.* Is it broken? I try to get to my feet, but my left one is the only one I can stand on, and even that one hurts. Walking doesn't seem to be an option.

I force myself into a crawl. Using my left elbow and knee, I drag myself through the rubble. The cat meows, as if cheer-ing me on. My legs scrape against all kinds of rough things, but I hardly feel them—I'm losing feeling more than gaining it. The spots around my vision don't fade. *Keep moving, keep moving.* A back door, half-open. Sunshine. Grass.

The fence. There. Seems miles away. Too much work.

The grass, so soft, I could just lie here...

A tongue licks my eyelids again. *Up, up. The cat wants you to get up.*

I drag myself along the grass. The door in the blue fence gets closer. Closer. I have to stop again and again because of the pain piercing through me. Somehow I'm within reach of the fence door now. Then next to it. I reach for the latch with my left hand. It won't budge. I squint, trying to see it through the dark spots in my vision. Is it rusted shut? I align my good eye with a slat in the fence. I glimpse some green—and that grayish blue—is that the creek? A brownish object sits on the grass—but I can't tell what it is. It could be the wheelbarrow, or a tree trunk...

I try the bolt latch again. It still won't slide. Tears fuddle what little I can see. I keep jerking, jerking, refusing to give up, even though this latch is clearly—

The bolt jerks all the way out and scrapes my knuckles against the wood of the fence. I tumble forward as the fence door swings open. *Ouch.*

I feel the cat brush past me.

I squint across the grass sloping down to the creek. And sure enough, there it is: the boat. The cat is wandering toward it.

I follow, pulling myself through the high grass, barely feeling it tickle me. The boat sits a few feet from the water. I reach up with my left hand and touch the wood—try to push.

It weighs a ton. I get onto my knees and push the boat closer to the water. I pause, wheezing.

The cat rubs against my thigh. I hoist myself up and clamber into the boat. It's filthy, I think, but I can't afford to care. I grasp for the oar and push it into the ground. My left arm trembles with the effort, but the boat is moving, sliding, rocking with my weight as it slips into the water. I can feel the lightness under me. This must be what it feels like to float.

I drop the oar and give the shore one more glance—the cat and the house watch me go. Then I drop onto my back, staring up into the sky, the clouds, as the current takes me away.

I drift in and out of consciousness, half-aware of the water sloshing on both sides of me, the birds crying above me. Coldness is all I feel, though I could have sworn it was a hot day. Coldness and the throbbing in my arm and leg. But soon I can't feel that either. My body seems to have detached itself and gone off somewhere. I try to keep my mind working so I don't go away completely. I imagine I'm drawing. I go through the pencil strokes, the lines, the curves of Grandma's face. The backs of my eyelids fill with them. Yes, the marks here for her nose, the shading there for her cheeks...

In an odd way, I'm neither awake nor asleep. Just drifting.

At some point, between the sloshes of water, I hear voices. Distant, then closer. Closer.

"Oh my god…"

"There's someone in there."

"Do you think they're…?"

"No, look, they're breathing."

"Quick, call 911."

I don't know what happens next, because the voices fade in and out. Everything feels too heavy now, looks too dark—as if my body held out just long enough to make sure I got to someplace where someone would find me. Someplace I wouldn't be if I hadn't remembered the photo—my mom's photo.

In a way, my mom saved me.

With that thought, I let it all go to black.

# PART III

RE·FLEC·TIVE

*adjective*

1. providing a reflection; capable of reflecting light or other radiation

2. thinking carefully about something; thoughtful

PART VII

# 24

B*EEEEP.*

    *Beeeep.*

*Beeeep.*

I know where I am before the second beep. I can feel bandages back on my face, a monitor clipped onto one of my fingers, and something stiff around my right arm and leg.

And a presence—a familiar scent. I open my eyes. It's her face. Yes, hers.

Grandma, doing one of her word search puzzles.

I clear my throat, not sure if I'm ready to form words yet. Grandma's eyes fly up, and she drops her pen, moving her hand onto mine. We look at each other. The creases around her mouth and eyes seem deeper than I remember.

"Hi, kiddo," she murmurs.

All the tears I've been holding back release themselves.

"Sshh." Grandma sits on the edge of the bed and leans forward, engulfing me. "It's all right."

"I'm sorry," I blubber into her shoulder.

She shakes her head. "You wouldn't have ended up in this hospital if it weren't for me. And whatever you saw out there—you weren't prepared. That's my fault too. Mine and Gladder Hill's."

I sniff. "You aren't mad I ran away?"

"No, no." She squeezes my hand. "I'm just glad you're okay."

I breathe in her scent.

"What happened out there?" she asks softly.

My time in Barkbee flashes through my mind in a blur. "I fell," I mumble.

"I could guess that much. You've sprained your ankle and elbow."

I look down for the first time since I woke up. My right arm's in a sling. The arm I write with—and draw with. A wave of sadness soaks me. Then it ebbs just as quickly. Maybe it's better that I can't draw for a while. Drawing is what got me into this mess.

"What I mean is, how did it happen?" Grandma says. "I only know what the police told me. You were with that girl, and then… How did you get into a boat?"

I take a deep breath. "I went to the house."

"The girl's house?"

She must mean Beryl. I shake my head. Then I recite the address—the address that held so much promise, so much hope for me just hours ago.

Grandma stiffens. "The police said they checked there."

I look her in the eye. "What happened in that house?"

Grandma blinks and looks down at her hand on top of mine. "What do you mean?"

"I know something happened there. Something bad."

She closes her eyes.

"You told me she abandoned me," I say.

Grandma winces. "Right. Poor choice of words on my part."

"It's not true?"

"Well, that's how I think of it when I feel angry. But the truth is I'm not sure who, or what, to be angry at."

"How'd she die?" My question comes out as a whisper. But I can't help asking. I need to know.

Grandma shakes her head, eyes still closed.

"I think I deserve to know. I'm not a little kid anymore."

At this she opens her eyes and looks me up and down, as if surprised to realize I'm right. "No, I guess you're not." She sighs. "Okay. All right. If you really feel the need to know... here goes. Your mother had an eating disorder."

I frown. "What does that mean?"

"It's a little complicated."

"Try me." I sit up as straight as I can in the bed.

Grandma rubs the back of her neck. "Let me put it this way. She couldn't stand what she saw in the mirror. It was never good enough. So she didn't eat. Exercised constantly. It became her top priority."

*She had other priorities—Superficial ones.* I remember the words Grandma said that time in the kitchen.

"I don't get it." I shake my head. "She died of..." I search for the right word. "Self-starvation?"

"Heart failure, technically," Grandma says. "Not eating made her heart weak."

The pieces start to fall into place. All at once it makes sense—why Grandma would always watch my dinner plate, always make sure I was eating... Those little moments as I grew up that I thought were just Grandma being Grandma.

"Was she always like that?" I ask.

"Not always, but..." Grandma pulls at a loose thread on my blanket. "She was only a little older than you when it started. Seemed better by college. But then she got pregnant.

And after you were born, the baby weight she'd put on just...
sent her into a relapse."

I feel the floor collapsing under me all over again. "She
died because of me?"

Grandma raises her eyebrows. "No—*no*. Did you hear
what I said? The problem started long before you were born."

"But she wouldn't have relapsed if—"

"*This* is why I didn't want to tell you." Grandma wrings
her hands. "It's not your fault. It's mine, if anyone's."

"Why would it be yours?"

She shakes her head. "Maybe there were things I said.
Compliments on her looks growing up..." She trails off. I find
it hard to believe that Grandma would ever have given compliments on looks. Avoiding them was a big part of interiority
lessons in kindergarten—we must have memorized at least
fifty compliments that have nothing do with appearance.
*You're so smart, so creative, so considerate...yadda, yadda,
yadda.* But then, Grandma must not have had those lessons
where she grew up.

She leans forward. "Do you see now why I jumped at
the chance to raise you in Gladder Hill? After what happened
to her, I never wanted anything like it to happen to you."
She hesitates. "That's why I got scared when I saw your

drawings. I worried that it had backfired. That you'd become just as fixated on looks..."

I cringe at the memory of my sketches. "I don't know why I drew them," I mumble. "I don't know what I was thinking."

"It doesn't matter right now, kiddo. I'm just sorry I overreacted the way I did." Water pools in Grandma's eyes.

She hugs me, and I let her scent fill my nostrils again— the scent of home.

Home. "I want to go home," I whisper, surprising myself. It's true: I'd dreamed of leaving Gladder Hill, and now all I want is to go back to what I know, our life, our house, my room, the familiar, the way things were...

Grandma hugs me tighter. "You got it, kiddo. We'll go as soon as the doctor gives us the green light."

Dr. Kahue presents the facts. My injuries from the fall should heal soon: an elbow sprain, a mild ankle sprain, minor cuts and scrapes, and some bruises. My injuries from the stove incident are more serious: I'm partially blind in my left eye, and as for my burns, he mentions a lot of things I don't understand and says that skin graft surgery is recommended for faster healing and minimal scarring. He doesn't explain what *skin graft* and *scarring* mean, but he glances at Grandma and tells her we don't have to make a decision right now. "Call me in a couple of weeks when the bandages come off," he says.

He fills us in on a few more things, like how the nurse in Gladder Hill will change my bandages in a week. And a week after that, when they come off, there's ointment I need to apply twice a day. All the information makes my head spin.

"And that's about it," Dr. Kahue says. "But before you go, I have to ask one more thing." He turns to me. "Just due to the nature of the situation, Zailey...did you see your reflection at all while you were out here in Barkbee?"

Both he and Grandma are watching me. I clear my throat. "A couple of times," I say.

Dr. Kahue nods and writes something on his clipboard. "Okay, and was that with your bandages on, or...?"

I hesitate. "Yeah. With them on."

Grandma's face doesn't change, but I swear her shoulders relax ever so slightly.

I decide not to say anything about the face in my mom's house. It happened so fast, and the mirror was so dirty, so blurry. I hardly know what I saw...

"Okay." Dr. Kahue is still writing. "I'm just asking

because normally we suggest patients like yourself get counseling to help you get used to your new appearance. But since you never knew your old appearance, and since you're going back to Gladder Hill anyway...it may be irrelevant for the time being." He looks at Grandma. "I trust the folks in Gladder Hill will know what's best for you."

Grandma cringed every time he said *appearance*, but at least she didn't interrupt him and storm out of the room this time. I can tell she's trying to cooperate. "Yes." She nods. "I think so."

The doctor's words bounce around in my head. *New appearance...old appearance...* That confirms it: I don't look the same as I did before the stove incident. If I ever see the mirror girl again, without the bandages, I'll still never know how she was before. I'll never know what other people saw when they looked at me all those years. That question will forever go unanswered...

But Dr. Kahue interrupts these thoughts, shaking Grandma's hand and my hand now and saying I'll be ready to go home in a few hours. Grandma steps out of the room to talk with Dr. Kahue outside, and I lie back, looking around the room and then down at my arm in the sling. I turn my free left hand over and stare at the smudged numbers still written there: Beryl's phone number.

*But you have to promise me something. That you'll let me know how it goes with your mom.*

I glance at the room phone on the little bedside table. I promised her…but that isn't what's niggling at me. Beryl made me a promise too. She said she wouldn't rat me out, but then she did. I just want to know why. Even though I don't have a mother outside of Gladder Hill, it would have been nice to at least have a friend—but I don't know if I can still call her one. I glance at the closed door and then pick up the phone, dialing Beryl's number quickly. I half expect it to not work, but it starts to ring. One ring, two rings, three… If the door opens, I'll just hang up.

"Hello?"

My stomach flips. That's definitely her voice.

"Hello?" she says again.

"Hey. It's Zailey."

"Oh my god. Are you okay?"

"Yeah, just a couple of sprains. No biggie."

"Where are you?"

"The hospital." I explain as best I can what happened after I left her house.

"I'm really glad you called," she says. "I've been wanting to say sorry."

"For what?"

"Telling on you. I kept thinking about the news, and once my mom mentioned it, I couldn't keep it in. I freaked—"

"It's okay."

"You don't hate me?" she says.

"No." I breathe out, realizing it's true. It was silly of me to be mad. Of course she acted out of concern, though at the time it felt like betrayal. I probably would have done the same thing if I were in her shoes.

"And *then* you weren't even in my room when the police came," she goes on. "I freaked out all over again. I think they thought I was making it up at first."

"Really, don't worry about it."

"Maybe I can come visit," she says. "How long will you be at the hospital?"

"A few more hours, the doctor said." I glance back at the door. "I should hang up now though. I don't think I'm supposed to be calling people."

"Wait. There's one more thing I need to tell you."

"What?" I keep an eye on the door.

Beryl hesitates. "My mom did something—I couldn't stop her. You have to understand, she'll do anything for her job, and—"

The doorknob turns. I slam the phone down.

The door opens, and Grandma walks back in. "There's someone here to see you, kiddo."

I blink, flustered by my secret phone call. "Who?"

Grandma half smiles. "It was a big deal for her to come. But she made arrangements as soon as she heard you were missing." Then she glances over her shoulder into the hall and nods. She steps forward, and a woman follows her into the room. The woman's wearing one of those surgical-type masks, covering everything on her face below her eyes. But her eyes...I know them. And her hair...it's buzzed. Like mine and Grandma's.

"How are you feeling, Zailey?" Principal Gladder says through her mask. "Sorry I didn't get here sooner." And it feels like two worlds are colliding.

# 25

PRINCIPAL GLADDER HAS TAKEN off her mask and now sits in the chair across from my bed, while Grandma goes down to the cafeteria to get bagels. It's weird being alone with Principal Gladder in a place that's not her office, and not in Gladder Hill for that matter. But then again, everything's weird lately.

"I hear you've had an adventure," she says.

"I guess that's one word for it."

She crosses her legs and hooks her folded hands around her knee. "Everyone back home was worried about you. First with the accident. And then when I got the call that you were missing." She reaches into her bag and pulls out some papers. "A lot of kids wrote you get-well cards."

I take them from her and scan them. Sorry to here about your axident, scrawled first grader Jeff Gallagher. Feel better soon! scribbled Malorie Windleson. MISS YOU AND HOPE YOU'RE OK! wrote Olive, with a bunch of hearts around it.

One card makes me grin: I hope your recovery is speed-ier than this guy, it says above a drawing of a turtle, or at least I think it's a turtle. I open the card. Inside, someone has written a whole paragraph. I check the name at the bottom— Noah. For some reason butterflies flutter in my stomach. I skim the letter.

Dear Zailey,

Mr. Grinwold is old news now thanks to you! You know how people here love having something to gossip about. Seriously, though, hope you're okay. Things have been weird since you left. After the helicopter picked you up, we had an assembly about you and everything. All the teachers are telling us not to worry, but... Just come back soon, okay? I have no one to talk to at the viewpoint...

Principal Gladder clears her throat, reminding me of her presence, and I stop reading. "Thanks," I say, tucking the card away to finish reading later. "And thanks for coming all the way here. You really didn't have to."

"This was a special situation."

"Sorry to cause so much worry." I feel a little queasy imagining her holding an assembly about me.

"I'm just glad you're okay." She pauses. "I heard you were looking for your mom."

I look down at my lap. "Well, I thought she was alive."

"Sorry you never got to meet her."

"It is what it is." I fiddle with a piece of lint on the hospital blanket.

Principal Gladder takes a deep breath. "I never knew your mom. But she and I are inextricably linked."

I look up at her. "What do you mean?"

"Your grandma told you what happened to her, right?"

"She died of an eating..." I forget the word Grandma used. "...problem?"

"An eating disorder." Principal Gladder nods. "I almost did too."

My fiddling fingers pause. "You had the same thing?" I can't imagine her ever having Superficial thoughts. She's Principal Gladder. She represents everything Gladder Hill stands for. Substance over surface.

"Well, the same diagnosis," she says. "I'm sure we had different experiences. Being a Hollywood actress probably didn't help mine." She snorts, and Beryl's TV screen flashes into my mind—the young woman in the "prom" movie. Then I blink, and the founder of Gladder Hill is back in front of me, her mask on the table next to her. The mask...why was she was wearing it anyway? I doubt it was germs she was avoiding. If she's as famous as I've heard, maybe the mask was supposed to protect her from being recognized. Or maybe…

*She couldn't stand what she saw in the mirror*, Grandma said about my mom. *So she didn't eat.*

Was it the same for Principal Gladder? Will her problem come back if she sees herself in a mirror?

A pang of guilt shoots through me. The only reason she left Gladder Hill's protection is because of me.

"Is it okay for you to be away from Gladder Hill?" I ask.

Principal Gladder smiles. "Don't worry, I put Ms. Mohill in charge. She'll keep the place running."

"No, I mean, is it okay for your…health?"

"Oh." Principal Gladder uncrosses her legs. "Yeah, it's fine. I've learned how to avoid triggers. I've come a long way, you know."

"That's good."

"Ten years ago it was a different story. And surviving that—well, it was like being born again. I had resources, so I thought maybe I could make a difference. Save lives."

"That's why you founded Gladder Hill?"

She nods. "I had high hopes too. Even with the criticism I got."

"What criticism?"

"Oh, you know." She waves a hand. "That Gladder Hill is too extreme. Or too exclusive. As if I *choose* to have limited space and resources. It's not like I haven't tried to get more funding, but it's almost always the same pushback: there are more pressing issues in the world than body image." She grunts. "Even though it's a national crisis. Especially for young people. That's why I hoped to expand one day." A shadow comes over her face. "But now...if it's not even working on a smaller scale..." Her shoulders slump.

I fidget. "But it *is* working...isn't it?"

She looks at me. "You tell me."

"Me?" I blink. "How would I know?"

She reaches into her bag and pulls something out. I can't tell what it is at first. It looks like trash. "After the helicopter picked you up, I came over to help Officer Jenkins clean the kitchen for your grandma." She sets the object on the bedside table. Then I see the burnt pages full of holes, the charred edges, the hint of an eye... My stomach turns at the sight of my handiwork. Grandma said she'd told everyone it was a cooking accident, but I guess Principal Gladder knows the truth.

"Please," I splutter. "Don't evict us." I hear the desperation rise in my voice. "I made a mistake. I—"

Principal Gladder holds up a hand. "Zailey, I'm not going to evict you."

"You're not?"

She sighs. "I need to recognize that maybe...Gladder Hill isn't working as well as I thought." She stares at the remnants of my sketchbook. "Mr. Grinwold was one thing, but you kids...you're the first generation to grow up here. I thought a controlled environment could keep you from caring about appearances. But maybe it's part of human nature. How can I fight that?"

*You kids?* Does she have reason to think other kids are Superficial too? Does she know about Noah? "I'm sure it's just me," I say. "I'm messed up."

She frowns. "Do you really think that?"

She tries to hold my gaze, but I drop my eyes and shrug. "Why else would I have Bad Thoughts?"

She doesn't say anything for a moment. Then she mutters something low that my ears barely catch: "What have I done?"

When I look up, the circles under her eyes seem to darken before me. "Maybe I made a mistake, creating a place like Gladder Hill." Her voice cracks. "I mean, it will never be perfect, but where is it even going? I was already having doubts before your accident. Maybe the system's hurting more than helping. Maybe…" She lets out a heavy breath. "Maybe it's time to close Gladder Hill."

I sit up in a panic. "Close? You can't close Gladder Hill." Words I never thought I'd utter to my own principal. But right now our roles feel reversed—like I'm the grown-up and she's the kid who needs to be reasoned with. What happened to confident Principal Gladder?

"Why not?" She slouches. "I'm not sure I see the point anymore."

"Because…" I search for the right words. "You can't just throw everyone out into the world with their reflections. People aren't ready. At least, I wasn't. Even if I thought I was."

She rubs her temples. "Right. But I've dug us into this hole—I'm not sure how to dig us out. Gradual exposure? But then I'll betray all the adults who moved there to get away from their reflections…" Principal Gladder shakes her head and waves a hand. "Sorry, Zailey. I shouldn't be burdening you with this. You've already been through so much. I'll figure it out." She moves to get up. "Why don't I—"

"You could start by giving us space," I blurt, surprising myself.

THE TOWN WITH NO MIRRORS

Her eyebrows rise. "Space?"

The idea is coming to me fast, but I want to make sure it comes out right, so I talk slowly. "Maybe if we each could have a space to talk to someone about our Superficial thoughts once in a while...that might help." I think of how good it was for me to talk to Noah about these things—how much it helped me work through my Superficial thoughts and feel less alone. And hadn't Dr. Kahue said something about counseling?

Principal Gladder sits back down and stares at me unblinking—until I squirm and wonder if I made a mistake in speaking my mind.

The door swings open. "Bagels!"

Principal Gladder and I both straighten.

Grandma sets a paper bag on the table. "They were out of poppyseed, Felicity, so I got you sesame."

"Mmm, perfect." Principal Gladder smiles. "Thanks, Hazel."

Grandma glances at the ruins of my sketchbook. "What have you two been talking about?" Her eyes swivel from the sketchbook to me to Principal Gladder.

I watch Principal Gladder, not sure what to do. Should I pretend the conversation we just had didn't happen? In the presence of Grandma—one of the many people who see her as a hero—maybe Principal Gladder will change her mind, want to keep her perfect image, regret confiding in me...

"Actually," Principal Gladder says, "Zailey was just sharing an excellent idea about how we can make Gladder Hill a better place." She shoots me a grin. "And I think it's worth a try."

# 26

I'M READY FOR DISCHARGE, the nurse says—a fancy way of saying I can't stay here anymore.

Beryl still hasn't visited the hospital, so I guess I won't be seeing her again. Maybe ever. It's probably for the best. What's the point in drawing out a friendship that can't last? It's not like we'll be able to hang out or communicate once I go back to Gladder Hill. Only a few important adults, like Principal Gladder and Officer Jenkins, have special phones that can make outside calls, and other adults need permission to use them; kids can't make outside calls at all.

The nurse helps me into a wheelchair, shows me how to use my good arm to propel the chair if I need to, and then rolls me out of the room. Principal Gladder has arranged for the Barkbee police to escort us home. Apparently the ride will take almost an hour. My body starts to tingle with excitement. I'm still not over the fact that I missed the helicopter ride over here, but I plan to stay conscious for this one—even if it's just a car this time.

"The car's waiting out front," the woman at the front desk tells us as we check out. Principal Gladder thanks her and the nurse; her mask is back on. Grandma isn't wearing one, but I notice she's keeping her gaze at her feet.

*Why would we want to watch ourselves grow old?*

Maybe my protection wasn't the only reason Grandma moved us to Gladder Hill. Does she have a complicated relationship with her reflection too? Another pang of guilt shoots through me. Has she glimpsed herself while she's been out here? Did she recognize herself in my face collection when she found it?

But now is not the time to bring that up.

Grandma rolls me toward the exit doors. As we pass the hospital convenience store, Principal Gladder stops us. "How about munchies for the road? My treat. It's the least I can do. You've been through a lot."

I grin and glance at Grandma, who gives a nod of approval.

"Pick out whatever you like." Principal Gladder walks into the little shop and beckons us to follow. "Candy? Chips? Something you think is scrumptious."

Grandma wheels me in, and I peer around at the snacks. They basically *all* look scrumptious.

"Oh wow, remember these?" Principal Gladder says to Grandma from the chips aisle, holding up a cylinder labeled *Pringles*. "I should see if I can get a shipment into Gladder Hill."

"Oh, I used to love those." Grandma goes over to look at them. "Once you pop, the fun don't stop." They laugh, sharing some sort of inside joke.

I use my good arm to wheel myself around the shop. Most of the candy is near the cash register. The woman behind it is chewing gum and perusing a booklet with photos all over it, only I can't see them well because she keeps flipping the pages. She has poofy purple hair and a ring around one of her nostrils. I didn't know it was possible for hair to be purple. And what's the nose ring for? Doesn't it hurt to have something sticking through your skin? She looks up and notices me staring. I flash an embarrassed smile and drop my eyes back to the candy. A rack next to it holds booklets kind of like the one the cashier is reading, with titles like *STARZ* and *PEOPLE DAILY*. The photos on the covers all show people: A woman in loose clothes walking somewhere as she eats a donut... A man with big shoulders hugging someone whose face he's blocking... And the photos are accompanied by headlines in big font.

Is Marly Pyros PREGNANT?

Ricky Stevens CAUGHT with another woman!

Botox AGAIN? Jenaya's fans worried she's gone too far

Felicity Gladder UNRECOGNIZABLE after 8 years hiding!

My heart catches in my throat.

I squint hard. But I'm not seeing things. It's my sketch—the one I did for Beryl yesterday—there, on the cover of a booklet, alongside a photo of a woman's face a lot like the one in that "prom" movie.

The word YIKES! in a little red circle connects the two images.

And below them, more text in smaller font:

Here's what she looks like now, according to inside source

My stomach turns. I thought I was giving my drawing to a friend.

Confusion and anger mix with panic. What if Principal Gladder sees these?

*I've learned how to avoid triggers*, she said. But what if this is a trigger she wasn't expecting?

I have no time to deliberate because I hear Grandma and Principal Gladder talking and laughing behind me. I glance at the cashier, who's still reading. Before I really know what I'm doing, I reach forward with my good arm and scoop the stack of booklets off the rack. I set the stack on my lap and propel my wheelchair forward, but the stack starts to tilt and slip, and I have to stop wheeling to catch it with my good arm. Grandma's and Principal Gladder's chatter gets louder—closer. There's no other way… I scoop up the booklets again, and then I'm out of my wheelchair, limping as fast as I can out of the shop.

"Hey!" I hear behind me. "You need to pay for those!"

In the lobby, people turn to look at me. The front doors aren't far; I break into a run. My sprained ankle throbs, but I need to get these booklets as far from Principal Gladder as possible. The automatic doors open for me, and I think I glimpse the mirror girl, but she's just a flash before I rush outside, bumping into someone and almost dropping the booklets.

"Whoa." Beryl stands before me, eyes wide. "I was just coming to visit you. What are you…?" She glances down at the stack of booklets in my arm. Her face falls. It's not a look of surprise. So she knew about the cover.

"How could you?" I mutter.

Beryl squeezes the straps of her backpack. The skin

under her eyes puffs out a bit, like maybe she didn't sleep last night. "I tried to tell you on the phone—"

"I thought I could trust you."

Her eyes fill with water. "It was my mom. She's a tabloid journalist, and she saw your drawing, and I told her I bought it from you, and the next thing I knew—"

"There's no time now." I look past her, though I'm not sure what I'm looking for. "I need to get rid of these." I hold up the stack of booklets. "Before Principal Gladder sees."

Beryl's eyes widen. "She's here?"

I should have kept my mouth shut. Maybe now she'll make things worse and try to get a new photo of Principal Gladder or—

"There—over there," someone shouts behind us. "She's stealing!"

Beryl and I both turn to see the purple-haired cashier pushing open the hospital doors, followed by a man with the word *security* on his shirt. Grandma and Principal Gladder are scurrying up behind them.

"Quick." Beryl taps me and points across the parking lot to a litter bin. "We can throw the tabloids in there. Come on." She starts running toward the bin. She wants to help me? Maybe she really is sorry. It isn't the best plan, but it will at least get the tabloids out of sight, and maybe no one will want to reach into the trash to get them back.

I start to chase after Beryl, but my limp slows me down. My ankle twinges. "Wait," I call. Beryl whirls around, and I hold out the stack of tabloids. "My ankle..."

"Zailey," Grandma shouts behind me. "Azalea, you stop right there."

Beryl dashes back to me and reaches for the tabloids. As I pass them to her, the security guard catches up to us and holds out a hand. "What's going on here? I heard you didn't pay for these." As Beryl and I exchange a *what do we do now?* look, a few tabloids slip from our grip, and the wind whips them away. One blows under a car, another dances toward the litter bin—go figure—and the other... I turn around and watch it skip back toward the hospital. I watch it the way I watched the leaflet skip toward me the day I met Beryl—only this time I'm watching with dread. This time I feel a mix of shame and self-loathing as it flaps against the ground near Principal Gladder's feet.

She pins it with her toe and bends to pick it up.

My gaze plummets to my arm in the sling. Suddenly I hope it never, ever heals. Because I would deserve it. And because in this moment I never want to draw again; I never even want to be tempted to.

There's a snort. "I see things haven't changed out here," Principal Gladder says.

I glance up to find her laughing through her mask and shaking her head at the tabloid. She hands it to the cashier, who mutters thanks, clearly unaware that the person standing in front of her is the same person on the cover.

A few other people have gathered outside the hospital, watching us. A police officer—where did he come from?— tells them there's nothing to see here, while the security guard takes the stack of tabloids from us. Beryl and I don't resist.

"She didn't do anything wrong, just so you know," I croak, gesturing at Beryl. "I'm the one who stole them. She shouldn't get in trouble."

"Yeah, I should," Beryl protests. "Because I—"

"You're lucky you're both off the hook this time," the guard interrupts. "Just don't let it happen again, okay?" He puffs out his cheeks and starts walking back toward the hospital. He stops in front of the doors and talks to the cashier and a nurse, who gestures at the tabloids and shakes her head. The guard nods, and the cashier shrugs, seeming to concede whatever they're arguing about. Then the guard tucks the tabloids under his arm, and the cashier follows him inside. Through the doors, I can see that the cashier turns right, toward the convenience store, but the guard walks straight ahead with the tabloids. Maybe they're not going back on display in the store after all. This might have felt like a victory if it had happened before Principal Gladder saw them. Keeping her from seeing them was all that mattered, and I failed big-time.

A hand touches my shoulder. "Time to go home now, Zailey." Grandma is by my side with my wheelchair. She doesn't scold me. She just nods her head toward the chair. In a daze, I let her nudge me into the seat. And as she wheels me away, I look back over my shoulder. Beryl is still standing by the litter bin, watching us go. She waves. I don't know if I'll ever see her again. And I still don't know if I can call her a friend. But I do know that, in the end, she tried to help me. In the end she was on my side. And maybe that means something good came from my otherwise disastrous trip to the outside world.

I wave back.

Grandma wheels me toward a parked car with black paint and black windows, not like the windows I've seen on other cars. Principal Gladder is already standing by the car, talking to a police officer and…laughing? She's not mad?

The officer—apparently our driver—opens the car

door, and Grandma helps me in. Then as the officer helps Grandma fold up my wheelchair and put it in the trunk, Principal Gladder slides into the seat on the other side of me.

"I'm really sorry," I blurt, before she can even close the door. "I never meant—"

Principal Gladder holds up a hand. "You don't need to explain. I could see you were trying to do the right thing. And really, I should be thanking you."

"*Thanking* me?"

She looks out the open car door toward the hospital. "Some things never seem to change out here. But I have. And it's nice to be reminded of that."

Grandma climbs into the car now, and Principal Gladder takes the middle seat. As the car pulls away from the hospital, Grandma presses a button on the handle of her door. The dark windowpane above it starts to roll down, and now the window is just an opening letting air in, like a Gladder Hill window. Principal Gladder leans over me and does the same on my door. Then the two of them start talking about how they're ready for a nap after all that excitement. I sneak a few more glances at Principal Gladder. She seems okay. Maybe she really is. Maybe some people, like my mom, don't heal, and maybe other people do—at least enough to keep living.

# 27

THE JOURNEY HOME FLASHES and flickers by the way dreams do. We are zooming past houses and buildings and fields and trees as the car speeds south, and the wind through the windows is keeping me cool. Grandma and Principal Gladder have kept the windowpanes rolled down the whole time. It can't be because of the heat—they could ask the driver to turn on the AC. No, I suspect that they have another reason. And that I won't get another glimpse of the mirror girl before I go back. The curious part of me is disappointed, but another part of me is relieved. And what would I see that's new anyway? My face is covered in bandages again.

I stare out in amazement at the scenery whizzing by: buildings, houses, yards, cars, road signs, and trees, interspersed with stretches of nothing—sweeps of sagebrush and rugged open spaces. Those stretches get longer the farther we go, and the landscape less green, but not less mesmerizing. Bike and golf cart rides in Gladder Hill can be nice, but nothing like this. There's so much to see out the car window that it distracts me for a while—until my eyelids blink and droop from overexcitement.

"Here we are, kiddo." Grandma's voice jolts me awake. "Home sweet home."

I blink sleepily and peer out the window. A hill rises before us. A tall fence surrounds it, but it crests high enough that I can make out a few streets running through it, stippled with houses. I've never seen Gladder Hill from the outside. An odd feeling comes over me. I've only been gone a couple of days, and I want Gladder Hill to feel exactly the same as when I left…but what if it doesn't?

The car pulls up to the front gates. Butterflies crowd my stomach as the driver helps Principal Gladder take my wheelchair out of the trunk. Then Grandma unfolds it and helps me into the seat. One of the security guards enters a code to open the gates for us. They part slowly, like I've seen them do a hundred times for the delivery trucks, only from the other side. Principal Gladder wheels me over the threshold, and suddenly an outburst of cheers fills my ears. I squint in the sun, trying to process what I'm seeing through my right eye.

WELCOME HOME, ZAILEY!

WE MISSED YOU

Get well soon

Everyone in Gladder Hill seems to be here, holding signs.

"Well, isn't this the sweetest," Grandma says next to me.

For a few seconds, I just stare, until Principal Gladder starts wheeling me down the drive. Everyone is a blur of smiles and hands waving, and all I can do is smile and wave back. It's like there's a screen between me and the rest of Gladder Hill—like I'm watching it all on Beryl's TV. Maybe it's the new issue with my vision. Maybe it's something else.

Either way, I'm home. I'm surrounded by familiar faces, familiar everything again. And I'm ready for things to get back to normal—if they even can.

I'm at the tree, picking peaches. I know I'm dreaming because the peaches are blue, very blue. This dream is weird: lucid, self-aware.

*Zailey!*

Someone's calling me from the house. I look up. The curtain in the upstairs window flutters. A hand pulls away.

*Zailey!*

I drop the peaches and run toward the house. Even

though it's a dream, I can't keep my heart from grinning. *Coming*, I call. *Be right there.*

I run inside and up the stairs to my mom's room. Except it isn't my mom's room, but a hospital room. I move past the hospital bed, over to the mirror on the wall, and look at the reflection there, the blurred, undefined face. No details. The figure makes all the same gestures I make, the same head and arm movements in reverse. I try to move fast, to surpass its imitations, because anything can happen in a dream, even outwitting a reflection.

I trick it a few times. I laugh.

The image shifts. The blurred face changes, sharpens, crystallizes. A creature looks back at me, and I don't understand what I'm looking at. I can't make sense of it.

One moment it looks like a Rubik's Cube, and the next like a floor tile, like curving petals within petals, orange and yellow lines, except now the lines start to move, to swirl with streaks of red that creep, branch, spread over the face in all directions. It makes me want to turn, flee, run far away.

Before I can, the demon's hand reaches out, breaks through the mirror, and grabs my arm.

There's no need to scream, because it's a dream.

But the demon's hand is turning my shoulder to ice. I don't like this dream.

I squirm, twist, try to break free. The hand pulls me forward. My face smashes against glass, through glass, through cold, all of me cold.

My body hits a hard surface. I groan and squint in sudden brightness. The room isn't right. Everything is made of mirrors—the walls, the floor, the ceiling. And the mirror demon is here. There. Everywhere. There are a thousand mirror demons.

On the ground lie a slingshot and a pile of small stones. The stones glimmer as if made of mirror too. I grab the slingshot. My aim was never good in real life, but it's superb now. I shoot at the demons, striking each one, stone by stone.

The problem is they won't die. Each demon I hit shatters to unveil another demon. Another mirror.

I look back at the mirror I came through. Inside it I see the room—only it's not the hospital room, but my bedroom with my desk and art posters. The mirror demon sits at the desk, drawing something, but I can't see what it is. I run up to the mirror and bang on the glass. The demon bares its teeth and waves at me.

Then it stands and walks away. I bang harder. It leaves

the room. I keep banging, but the glass won't break, won't crack, won't let me out of here...

"Kiddo?"

I jolt up in bed, sticky with sweat.

"It's all right." Grandma is by my side. I must have cried out. "Are you feeling okay?" she says.

"Yeah. Just a bad dream."

"Here, have some water." She hands me a cup. I'm glad she doesn't ask what the dream was about. I'm not sure I'd know the answer.

I drain the cup through the spout, and then she holds out a package. "Here's something else for you."

I stare at the polka-dot wrapping paper. "What is it?"

"You'll know when you open it."

I tear away the gift wrap to find a new sketchbook. I frown at Grandma, remembering how mad she was when she found my last one. How the world turned upside down after that...

"For when your arm heals," she says.

I shake my head. "I'm done drawing. Even when my arm gets better, I'm done."

Her brow furrows. "But you love to draw."

"Not anymore."

Grandma leans forward. "Listen, kiddo. I saw your drawings that day. And even though I was focused on the subject matter, I can't deny they were good. Your mom would be proud to know you got the artistic gene. She was an artist too."

"You mean her photography?"

"You know about that?"

I hesitate. "I found the photo. With the puppy."

Grandma brightens. "You have it?"

My stomach twists. She must have been looking for it. And she doesn't know. How can I tell her?

But the guilt is too much now. "It was inside my sketchbook," I say. I can't look at her.

"Oh."

"I'm really sorry."

Grandma shifts on the bed. I listen to her silence. It feels like ages till she speaks again. "Well, I wasn't even supposed to have it here. That was the hardest part of moving to Gladder Hill. Not being allowed to keep photos."

"None at all?"

"None. Especially not of people. Not even lost loved ones. Not even my daughter."

"Because it's Superficial?"

Grandma runs her fingers along the side of my comforter. "That's what the rule book would say. But when you miss someone..." She shakes her head. "I don't think it's Superficial to want to see someone you love and miss."

I remember how I felt when I thought I was dying. I thought of Grandma's face...and that didn't feel Superficial.

"So you had to throw away all your photos of her?" I say. "That doesn't seem fair."

"I'm sure your mother would have liked me to. She hated photos of herself. But I couldn't do it. I sent them to a friend of hers in Wyoming."

My skin tingles. Photos of my mom exist?

There's something about knowing that—just having the awareness that they're out there somewhere, in Wyoming, wherever that is, and that maybe I could see them one day... know what she looked like...

But do I want to know? Does it matter? I guess I have time to decide. For now, I like thinking of her as that photograph she took. That happy scene...

"I wish we still had the one with the puppy," I say. "It gave me this feeling—like warm fuzzies."

Grandma smiles. "Yeah. It was nice, wasn't it? It was...
beautiful."

I raise my eyebrows. *Beautiful.* That word from the list
on Beryl's leaflet. Her eyes twinkle as they meet mine, as if
to say, *Yes, you heard right. I'm using that word.* I never got a
chance to look up the definition. But I think I'm starting to get
the gist.

"She had an eye for landscapes," Grandma goes on. "For
capturing scenery that made you feel something. Photography
was an outlet for her, a way of exploring her thoughts about
the world around her. And if drawing helps you in a similar
way..." She taps my new sketchbook. "If it helps you sort
through your thoughts and questions, then who am I to take
that away from you?"

I look from her to the sketchbook and flip through
its crisp, blank pages, all waiting for the tip of my pencil.
"Well...I guess there's plenty to draw besides faces."

Grandma takes a deep breath. "What you decide to draw
in it, as an artist, is up to you. That's no one else's business."

I glance back at her. I can't believe the words I'm
hearing out of her mouth. Is she saying it's okay for me to
draw faces?

She shrugs, as if reading my thoughts. "You're the one

who told me you're not a kid anymore, right? But I just need you to remember one thing—no matter what happens in the future."

"Okay," I say. "What?"

"What you look like is one thing, and who you are is another."

# 28

M Y ANKLE IS ALREADY feeling better, but Grandma and
Principal Gladder both agree that I should stay home
from school for the next week. I have no complaints about
this staycation—a silver lining.

That is, until I realize I'm still expected to do homework.

Principal Gladder said a volunteer would bring me my
assignments. I wasn't sure who would volunteer. I guess I
had someone in mind—but it wasn't Olive.

"Hi." Her heart-shaped face appears in my doorway.
"Can I come in?"

"Of course."

She smiles and sits next to me on the edge of the bed.
"I brought your makeup work." She sets a stack of papers on
the desk.

"Thanks. Did I miss a lot?"

"Nah." She glances at my face bandages and then my
arm sling. "But I hear you've *been through* a lot."

I'm not sure how much she knows. I nod. "Yeah, but I'm okay now."

"That's good." She swings her legs back and forth and looks around my room. When was the last time she was in here? It's been a while since she decided she didn't want to be my best friend. She clears her throat. "I was really worried about you. The cooking accident sounded...scary."

Cooking accident—right. She doesn't know what really happened. Would she be here if she knew the truth?

She takes a deep breath. "I'm glad you're back, because I've been thinking while you were away. I want to say sorry."

"Sorry for what?"

"I shouldn't have accused you of being Superficial. I know you're not like that." She smiles. "I'd love it if we could be good friends again."

I stare at her. "It wasn't a cooking accident," I say.

She frowns. "It wasn't?"

If Principal Gladder knows the truth, there's no reason Olive shouldn't. Especially if she really wants to be "good friends." So I tell her. I explain my face collection and how it led to the fight with Grandma and the fire. It pours out of me practically in one breath, and then I wait. I wait for her to tell me she understands, like Beryl did when I told her.

Instead, her friendly smile vanishes.

I can feel the distance between us stretching. She gives me the coldest look and then stands. "I should go."

I don't stop her. Because even though it makes me sad, I know now that what she claimed to want—for us to be "good friends" again—can't happen. At least not while she holds herself so far above me.

But I have to hand it to her for being such a good Gladder Hillian—or at least seeming to be. I wonder what Principal Gladder would think to know she's created someone who might be an even bigger stickler for the cause than she is.

It turns out I'm not very good at staycations, because after just a couple of days in the house, I itch to get outside. Grandma still thinks I shouldn't walk much on my ankle, even though it feels fine now, so I wait until she's out running an errand before I put on my sun visor and walk to the viewpoint. It's only ten minutes from the house, so hardly a trek. It feels good to be out and about and moving my legs again. I whistle as I walk, carrying my new sketch-book in my good arm. When I crest the hill, the landscape opens before me as it always has. I stare out at the fields and roads and strip of river reaching toward the north. Even with my left eye partially blind, I can still see the horizon. It's weird looking at it all now, having been out there. Is that Barkbee, I wonder—that cluster of stuff near the horizon? Is that where I had my big adventure?

For all I know, it can't even be seen from here.

I sit cross-legged in the brown grass and open my sketchbook. I've been easing back into drawing, even if it means experimenting with my left hand, since my right arm is still in a sling. The results look like the work of a five-year-old, but it feels good to be creating again—and who knows, maybe I can become ambidextrous.

I'm not ready to get back to drawing faces, but I've been doodling some other stuff that I used to draw, like stars and mountains and flowers. I'm also working on re-creating my mom's photograph. I can't replace the original, but I can bring it back in some way—even add my own touches. Right now, I add the orange-and-white cat, sitting by the open fence door, so that the puppy can have a friend, and because I wish I could thank him for helping me. Maybe this is why people still draw; sure, photography may capture things exactly as they look in a given moment, but that also limits it.

The sound of padding feet startles me. I close my

sketchbook—it must be an instinct, left over from my face collection days.

Noah's Pop Eyes appear, coming up from the opposite direction. He stops a few yards away and waves. "I wondered if I'd find you here."

"I guess some things didn't change while I was gone," I say. "This is still the best spot in Gladder Hill."

"Yeah, it was weird sitting up here without you."

"You came up here?"

"A few times." He puts his hands in his pockets. "I kept looking out, wondering if I happened to be staring at the exact spot where you were." He laughs. "I don't even know where Barkbee is."

I look out to the north. "Me neither. Maybe it's that cluster near the horizon."

"That's where I kept looking."

"Really?"

We glance at each other at the same time. He coughs. "Anyway, glad you're back. And did you hear Mr. Grinwold's moving back?"

I grin. "Yeah. Return of the pinwheels!" Grandma just told me this morning that the new family who was supposed to move in got put back on the waiting list.

Noah laughs again and sits next to me. We stare out in silence for a minute.

"I wanted to volunteer to bring your homework," Noah says, "but I figured your grandma still doesn't like me at your house."

"Don't worry, she's over it now. I think she got some perspective while we were out there." *I did too*, I almost say—but I'm still working out what that perspective is.

"What was it like out there?" he asks. "You don't have to talk about it if you don't want to."

I hesitate. There was so much I wanted to tell him about while I was in Barkbee—windows, TV, the internet, the books, all the faces…and of course mirrors. But I'm trying to get back to my old life in Gladder Hill, to feel back to normal, and if I bring all that up now… I sigh. "I'm not sure I'm ready yet. I think I'm still processing it all."

He nods. "That's cool."

I wonder if he's going to lose interest in me now—if that's the real reason he came up here looking for me—to find out about Out There. It occurs to me he may have been using me from the start. Isn't that the reason he started hanging out with me more before my accident? He wanted someone to draw him, someone to talk to about Out There, someone willing to let him look into their pupils long enough to maybe see himself...

And that's why I hung out with him too. Isn't it? It was mutual. But that's not friendship. I tricked myself into thinking it might be, when we were only bonding over our Superficiality...

"Wanna play?" Noah interrupts my reverie. He's holding up a deck of UNO cards.

I blink. "Oh—sure." Then I remember... "Just one problem." I point to my arm in its sling.

He shrugs. "So? I'll play with my left hand too."

I raise a skeptical eyebrow under my bandages, but he goes ahead and deals the cards with his left hand, fumbling. As we play, we keep dropping cards and can barely go ten seconds without laughing. Neither of us mentions our unfinished plans from before. I think we both know there's no point: my drawing arm is out of commission for now, and my face bandages are still on. I can't draw him, and he can't draw me.

And I'm not sure I'll be ready to finish those plans even when the bandages come off.

# 29

THE NURSE COMES OVER to change my bandages Monday morning—right before my first day back to school. I've been home for a week now, but the bandages feel like they've been on for weeks, *plural*.

I sit on the hamper in the bathroom while Miss Ellowby removes the old dressings, following the Barkbee doctor's instructions. I can't bring myself to watch her face—to see how she reacts. Or to risk glimpsing someone in her pupils.

After she pulls the last bit off, all she does is nod and say, "Great, now for the ointment." She hands me a tube of the stuff. She wants me to apply it so I can get used to doing it myself. I wash my hands and rub it on. The texture under my fingers shocks me at first, even though I've felt it once before, on that strange walk from Beryl's house to 6 Creekside Road.

But I don't let my fingers dwell since Miss Ellowby is watching.

She puts on the fresh bandages, enwrapping my face once again. "We'll take these off in another week," she tells me.

Then we go to the kitchen where Grandma is waiting to offer Miss Ellowby some breakfast, and they chat a bit before Miss Ellowby heads out and I have to get ready for school.

"Are you sure you feel up to it, kiddo?" Grandma hovers around me as I tie my shoes. "I think Principal Gladder would understand if you took more time before you go back."

"I'm fine." I smile, even though my stomach is dancing with nerves. I don't know why; it's just school. There's no point in falling even more behind with schoolwork, and besides, it's a little boring sitting around the house. Better to get back to normal sooner rather than later.

But maybe that's part of what I'm worried about— will it even feel "normal"? I'm wearing face bandages; that's obviously not normal, even though no one is supposed to care, or at least show that they care. I can already imagine every-one trying to act like they don't notice them. And whisper-ing about me or just straight-up interrogating me about my adventure because it's the most exciting thing to happen to any of us.

I won't know how it will be till I get there, but I'm at

least glad that Noah is meeting me at the viewpoint to walk with me from there. He knows I'm a little nervous, and maybe not walking into school alone will help.

"Just take it easy, okay?" Grandma hands me my lunch bag. "And tell your teacher if at any point you don't feel well." She kisses me on the forehead before I head out the door.

Outside, someone is gardening next door.

I hover in front of the house. "Hi, Mr. Grinwold."

He looks up from his coneflowers.. "Oh. Howdy, Zailey."

"Welcome back."

"Well, thanks. And same to you. Are you feeling better?"

"Making progress."

"That's good."

There's an awkward pause. Mr. Grinwold puts down his garden trowel and sits back on his heels. "Listen, Zailey, I'm sure you've heard some things about me..."

I shake my head. "You don't have to explain." I do want to know more, I'll admit, but I can tell this is hard for him to talk about. And he's already said more to me in this conversation than in any we've had before.

"Right, well, I hope you don't think less of me." He looks down at his dirty gardening gloves. "I really wanted living here to help me. Still do. But…I found it hard going cold turkey at first. So I…well, I'm not the perfect resident…" He trails off.

"I'm not either." I shrug. "Maybe none of us are."

He exhales and smiles.

"The new pinwheels look great," I say. And with that, I wave and head off, silently asking Mother Nature to send a little breeze Mr. Grinwold's way.

The sun is shining, but the morning air is still cool. I breathe in deep. Walking to school does make the world feel sort of back to normal. The nightmares have been happening less often too. Of course, some things are different, in a good way: Principal Gladder has already implemented some of my suggestions into the community—counseling sessions for discussing Superficial thoughts, which she's now acknowledged as normal, even healthy, in moderation. My first session was yesterday with Principal Gladder and Noah, and we talked and journaled for almost an hour. It felt good.

I reach the viewpoint before Noah does, taking in everything before me, every field and road and cluster of buildings my good eye can see, until I hear Noah's feet padding.

"Fancy meeting you here," he says.

I smirk. "You're two and a half seconds late." I expect him to make a witty comeback, but instead he's staring at me, his Pop Eyes widening and then bulging.

My ears burn. Did the nurse not cover all of my face with the new bandages? Is he seeing some of it? Now every part of me wants to turn and run back home.

"Holy smoke." He raises his arm and points. It takes me a second to realize that both his gaze and his finger are fixed on something past me.

Relief loosens my shoulders, but only a little, because his expression still worries me. I turn around, taking in the view toward the south horizon. Only it's not the usual view.

Black clouds rise from the sagebrush and trees in the distance, mixing with orange flames.

All my breath leaves me. I haven't seen fire since that day...

"Holy smoke, holy smoke," Noah repeats.

I blink and try to even out my breathing. No flames are clawing at my face. The fire of the past is out.

But here in the present, there's a new one to deal with.

"What is that?" Noah mutters behind me. "Do you think it's a wildfire?"

I squint at the far-off blaze, and all I can think of is the phrase *spread like wildfire*. That seems to rouse me from my stupor. I whirl toward Noah, who's still gawking ahead. "Maybe no one else has noticed it yet," I say. "We have to tell someone." I grab his arm and pull him after me.

We sprint down the hill to downtown. I jab the doorbell at the police station, breathing hard. Noah bangs on the door. Officer Jenkins is taking forever to answer. Maybe he isn't even in yet; it's early.

"Should we try his house?" Noah says.

But then the door opens, and words come tumbling out of Noah and me. "Wildfire—smoke—south—"

"Whoa, whoa, slow down, kids." Officer Jenkins holds up a hand and yawns. "You're gonna have to talk properly so I can understand you. I haven't had my coffee yet."

He's used to business as usual. Nothing to worry about except the occasional kitchen fire. I almost feel bad that we're about to disrupt his routine. And maybe all of Gladder Hill's.

But something tells me this can't wait.

The next fifteen minutes are a blur of chaos.

First, Noah and I bring Officer Jenkins up to the

viewpoint to show him what we saw. He squints at the fire for a moment before whipping out his walkie-talkie. "Hey, Felicity? It's Greg. Can you meet me at the station ASAP?"

We follow him back to his office, mostly because we want to know what's going on, and he's too distracted to stop us. Next, he calls some outside number on his office phone—I can tell because he dials a few extra numbers, and his is one of the few adult phones that can make outside calls. He reports the wildfire, and whatever the person on the other end tells him makes his lips go thin.

Then Principal Gladder bursts into the office, wearing a wrinkled *Everyone's gladder in Gladder Hill* shirt backward. She glances quizzically at Noah and me, and that's when Officer Jenkins remembers us and asks us to go wait in the hall. We hover outside the door, straining our ears to try to catch what they're saying.

Something makes Principal Gladder raise her voice. "What? No. No way." Her pitch sounds higher than usual. "This is a controlled environment. Once we all leave—"

"I know. But it's either that or risk everyone's lives. Fires like this spread fast, and we don't know how long it will take to put it out. Our fences aren't going to keep it out if it reaches here."

There's a stretch of silence. Noah and I press our ears to the door.

Then I think I hear Principal Gladder sigh. "Well. I gave it my best shot." Her voice cracks. "Let everyone know we're evacuating."

Noah's eyes meet my good one and widen. Evacuating? He must feel it too—a change in the air. In the world as we know it.

At the same time, I catch a flash of something in his pupils. The tiniest bandaged head—

I look away, my heart racing.

"It'll be okay," Noah whispers. He must detect the worry on my face, or what he can see of my face.

I nod and manage to smile—even though I know that once we leave here, for who knows how long, it will be harder to avoid the mirror girl—and whatever I glimpsed in my mom's cracked mirror. I'll never be able to fully hide from her.

But maybe facing her is better than hiding. Because what is Gladder Hill if not a hiding place? Ridiculous as that tabloid headline was—FELICITY GLADDER UNRECOGNIZABLE AFTER 8 YEARS HIDING!—maybe the *hiding* part had a point. What else are the gates and rules and bans for, except to hide us from parts of ourselves—even if those gates and rules and bans were made with the best intentions?

As Principal Gladder and Officer Jenkins mumble behind the door, a hand slips into mine.

My stomach somersaults. My palm tingles with warmth.

Noah swallows. He's scared too, I realize—maybe more than I am. I'd like to think we're all a little more prepared to leave Gladder Hill now than we might have been, thanks to the new counseling sessions, but they only just started. I have a feeling we're going to need a lot more on the other side. Especially if we ever want to look in each other's eyes without looking for ourselves first.

"Yeah," I whisper. "We'll be okay." Then I squeeze Noah's hand, and he squeezes back, as sirens start to blare.

# EPILOGUE

Excerpt from the *Barkbee Herald*:

## NEW EXHIBITION TO OPEN AT SOUTHWEST HERITAGE MUSEUM

The Southwest Heritage Museum has announced a new exhibition opening next week. Set to be a permanent installation, it will showcase the history and culture of the now-defunct Gladder Hill community.

After last year's wildfire damage, founder and former movie star Felicity Gladder decided not to resume Gladder Hill operations, which had lasted for nearly nine years, but this exhibition allows the community's unique story and mission to live on.

Curated by Gladder herself, the exhibition showcases everything from artifacts to artwork, and all proceeds will go toward her new foundation for people battling eating and body image disorders.

A highlight of the exhibition is an art collection called "The Faces of Gladder Hill" by young artist Zailey S., who grew up in Gladder Hill and suffered facial burns at age twelve. This set of 103 hand-drawn portraits depicts all former Gladder Hill residents, including a self-portrait.

"It was a step toward acceptance and healing for me," Zailey said of the latter.

We could try to describe the collection here, but that might defeat the purpose; you really ought to see it for yourself.

# AUTHOR'S NOTE

Gladder Hill came from my imagination; I don't know of any such community in real life. That said, it has a number of real-life inspirations.

Before I get to those, though, I ought to mention a not-so-real-life inspiration—because while you might see no trace of it in the finished book, this novel began with a fairy tale. Many years ago, I found myself thinking about Snow White's happily ever after. It occurred to me that Snow White might have wanted to ban mirrors from her kingdom as soon as she became queen. After all, she'd almost died at the hands of a mirror-obsessed stepmother. Then I began to imagine what such a society would be like—one without mirrors or any reliable way of knowing what your face looks like. Would it be a utopia as intended? Or would it actually feel like a dystopia?

But Snow White wasn't my only consideration as this idea brewed—and this is where the real-life inspirations come in. On a personal level, I'd had my fair share of body image issues growing up, and I'd spent a lot of time in front of mirrors—time I could have spent on more fun or fulfilling activities. Modern America's unrealistic physical ideals make mirrors—and, by extension, cameras and anything else that helps us fixate on our looks—more hazardous to our mental health than ever. They can certainly facilitate body dysmorphic disorder, eating disorders, and other conditions that can affect anyone from a young age. It shocked me to learn over time how many people I knew who had, like myself, struggled with disordered eating as a teen, whether clinically diagnosed or not. And, while media and beauty standards are a huge part of the problem, I couldn't help wondering if the world would be a happier place without mirrors, cameras, and the like. Physical comparison would at least become harder to do.

With this question in mind, I searched online to see if any government or society had ever banned mirrors and specular materials. I couldn't find anything in that regard, but I did come across mirror fasting, a trend that had gained popularity among American bloggers in 2012. It involved abstaining from looking at one's reflection for an extended period of time, whether that was a day or a year, as an experimental attempt to improve body image. While such an endeavor seems helpful in theory, some people have argued that mirror fasting actually intensifies the fixation on one's appearance. I realized that the fictional society I'd been envisioning takes the mirror fasting trend to an extreme and that this extreme could provide a new lens for exploring the mental and societal ramifications of physical ideals. I also more recently realized that the overall aims of my well-intentioned fictional society felt somewhat in line with the rising body neutrality movement, an alternative to the better-known body positivity movement.

While my story idea initially manifested as a sequel to Snow White, the premise felt even more impactful when I started to rewrite it in a contemporary setting. Perhaps that's because the modern world presents so many more opportunities for physical comparison than the fairy-tale world of Snow White. Along with the increased use of video calls recently— which has meant frequently seeing our own face next to others—our lives have been riddled with selfies and profile photos, not to mention photo IDs, for a while now. So it can feel like one's face is irrevocably linked with one's identity. Even Zailey feels this to a degree, despite Principal Gladder's efforts to separate the two in Gladder Hill.

Needless to say, it can be easy to confuse what you look like with who you are—to feel like your face and body define you, even when you know they shouldn't. If you are grappling with this, you're by no means alone. And if you are struggling with your body image and mental health, know that help and support are available. Check out the following websites for more information.

National Eating Disorders Association:

www.nationaleatingdisorders.org

Child Mind Institute:

www.childmind.org

Anxiety and Depression Association of America:

www.adaa.org

# ACKNOWLEDGMENTS

No words can reflect (pun intended) my gratitude for all the incredible people who helped me to get to this point, where I can write acknowledgments for a second book. "Sophomore novel syndrome" was all too real for me, so for a long time I doubted I'd ever get here. I did in the end, but not without help.

Thank you to my agent, Becky Bagnell of the Lindsay Literary Agency, who has championed my work for years now and is always ready to help me in whatever way she can; my editor at Sourcebooks, Wendy McClure, who so welcomingly adopted me as one of her authors, provided brilliant manuscript notes, and guided me through the production process; Molly Cusick, who saw potential in my book proposal and sample, set this book on its publication journey, and gave insightful feedback on the first draft; Kate Prosswimmer, whose advice on a very early proposal helped steer the novel in a better direction; Alexandra Devlin and Rights People, who have looked out for me stateside; and Chelsey Moler Ford, Julie Larson, Maryn Arreguín, and everyone else on the Sourcebooks Young Readers team who helped turn *The Town with No Mirrors* into a finished book.

I also want to thank everyone who gave feedback on my fictional mirrorless community before it even became Gladder Hill in a contemporary novel. These folks include my husband Rory, Courtney Brkic, Erica Little, Lauren Buckley, Monica Boothe, and fellow MFA workshop participants at George Mason University.

Last but definitely not least, I'm grateful to my friends and family, including my ever-encouraging parents and little brother, for cheering me on. A special thank-you goes to my husband, who has cooked me so many fueling meals and been an all-around supportive presence in my life.

# ABOUT THE AUTHOR

Christina Collins grew up in Massachusetts, devouring books, looking for secret gardens, and using "wicked" as an adverb. She holds a PhD from Queen's University Belfast and an MFA from George Mason University, both in creative writing, and lives in Northern Ireland with her husband and son. Her debut novel, *After Zero*, was a 2019 NCTE/CLA Notable Children's Book in the Language Arts. Visit her website at www.christinacollinsbooks.com.